ABORTED RESCUE . . .

The pilot's voice came distorted and faint against the roar: "Three hundred meters up, and your reflector is shining loud and clear. Hold on, gang." The shuttle's thirty-meter bulk hovered, then slowly descended. The snowstorm was literally blown away around it, and looking up, Bjault could see the hillsides lit by painfully bright, electric-blue light. He gasped. They *had* been followed: across the snowfields, dozens of figures stood silhouetted in the glare.

The craft lurched slightly, then toppled to one side. Draere's voice came as calmly as if she were discussing ancient history. "Ground turbulence like I've never seen. I can't recover . . ." The blunt-nosed ferry curved gracefully downward, smashed sideways into the valley floor, and exploded. . . .

Yoninne had just risen to her knees, her machine-pistol coming to bear on the three soldiers, when a thunderlike snapping sound shook the ground and she was thrown head over heels into the snow behind her.

The men and women of Planet Earth have just received their introduction to the power of mind.

This edition contains fifteen full-page illustrations by award-winning artist Doug Beekman.

Books by Vernor Vinge

The Witling

Vernor Vinge

A Tom Doherty Associates Book • New York

This is a work of fiction. All the characters and events portrayed in this novel are either fictitious or are used fictitiously.

THE WITLING

Copyright © 1976 by Vernor Vinge

Originally published in 1976 by DAW Books.

Illustrations copyright © 1986 by Doug Beekman

Map of Giri drawn by Vernor Vinge. Map copyright © 1976 by Vernor Vinge

A Tor Book
Published by Tom Doherty Associates, LLC
175 Fifth Avenue
New York, NY 10010

www.tor.com

Tor® is a registered trademark of Tom Doherty Associates, LLC.

Library of Congress Cataloging-in-Publication Data

Vinge, Vernor.
    The witling / Vernor Vinge. —1st ed.
        p. cm.
    "A Tom Doherty Associates book."
    ISBN-13: 978-0-765-30886-3
    ISBN-10: 0-765-30886-X
        1. Life on other planets—Fiction.   2. Human-alien encounters—Fiction.
    3. Psychokinesis—Fiction.   I. Title.
    PS3572.I534W58 2006
    813'.54—dc22   2006048189

First Tor Edition: December 2006

Printed in the United States of America

0 9 8 7 6 5 4 3 2 1

To Joan D. Vinge, for all her support
in the writing of this novel

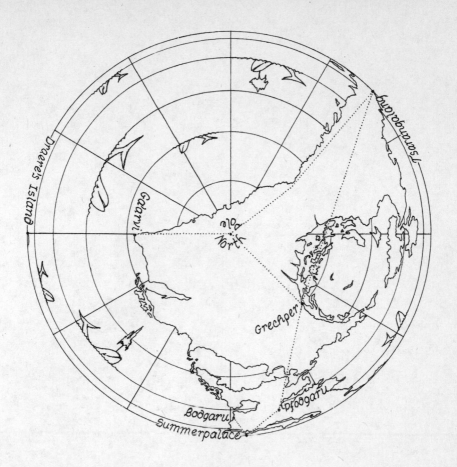

York

Draeve's Island

Galavi

Tsannobianna

Grechper

Bodgaru

Summerpalace

Pfoogaru

GIRI

NORTHERN HEMISPHERE VELOCITY FIELD

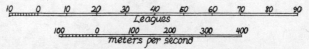

(Drawn in the manner of an Azhiri navigation
map. Dotted lines represent major roads.)

— A. Bjault

The Witling

One

Fall had come to Bodgaru-by-the-Sea, and winter was not now far away. All up the sides of the mountains that sheltered Bodgaru's northern flank, the tri-crowned pines stood green and snowy white in the fading sunlight. The town itself was still free of snow, but the cutting edge of the sea wind blew up off the beaches to lay sand and dust across the frosted brown grass that separated the townspeople's stone houses. Only the furry terns were about in the out-of-doors these days: they screaked and scrawked as they glided between the houses. The townspeople were Summerfolk, and when the weather turned cold, many of them moved south where summer was forever. Those who stayed kept indoors, and worked their mines buried thousands of feet within the mountains.

Parapfu Moragha looked out upon the scene, and silently cursed the day he had been appointed prefect of Bodgaru. Oh, at the time it had seemed quite a coup. His stone manse sat large and imposing on the ridge line that shielded the terminus of the Royal Road from the mountains to the north; he ruled a land larger than some duchies. But his vast "domain" was a cold, ugly borderland of the Summerkingdom. Bodgaru was seven leagues north of the equator—a short ride on the road, but more than two thousand miles as pilgrims walk it. The glaciers and mountains and snow-covered deserts that stretched from Bodgaru away to the North Pole were all claimed by the Snowking.

Moragha turned away from the thick quartz window to eye his visitors with barely disguised distaste. A half-wit, a Guildsman, and a common miner. It was outrageous that he should be bothered by the likes of these on the eve of the prince-imperial's visit, a visit that might be his last chance to persuade his friends at court to get him a new assignment. He eased himself onto the fur cushions that covered his stone chair, and said, "Really, Prou, why *are* you here?"

Thengets del Prou returned his accusing look with characteristic blandness. Only the glint in his eyes told Moragha that the tall, dark-skinned Guildsman was really laughing at his discomfiture. "I am within my covenanted territory, My Lord. Bodgaru is less than eight leagues from Dhendgaru."

Theso Lagha, first speaker of the miners' association, bobbed his head respectfully. He, at least, showed proper courtesy. "I asked him to come here tonight, My Lord Prefect. It seemed to me that what Hugo saw was important, so important that you might need the Guild immediately."

Moragha grimaced. Covenant or no, he feared the Guild. And he trusted Prou even less than the average Guildsman; the dark-faced smart aleck was of desert stock, with a practically unpronounceable name. Moragha wished that the miners didn't need Prou's senging quite so often, that the

Guildsman would stick to his assigned city. "Very well, good Theso, just what did your man see?"

Lagha urged the third visitor toward Moragha's throne. "Yes, My Lord. Hugo here is indentured to our association as a woodcutter. Tell My Lord Prefect what you saw, Hugo."

Hugo was obviously a half-wit and a witling. His eyes wandered aimlessly about the room as he fiddled nervously with the sewn bladders of his slicker; Lagha and Prou at least had the grace to leave theirs by the pool. After several incoherent garglings, the old man finally managed: "May it please M'lord, I cut wood . . . for freeman and his friends, them that pull the rock from the hills. Mostly, I cut tri-crown pine over . . . over . . ."

"Over northeast of town, away from the prospecting hills," put in Lagha.

"Yea . . . nice up there. No people. No things, excepting paddlefeet sometimes . . . and that only after the snow comes all the way into town. . . ." He paused for a long moment but his owner did not prod him on. Finally he recovered his chain of thought. ". . . But this last nineday, before the first snow, there's been some . . . thing so strange up there. Lights, faint. Like you see over Bilala's marsh at night sometimes in the summer. I thought it might be same thing, but no, the lights stay and stay. Pretty. I go closer last night. Come in from the north. . . . Quiet, quiet. There are people there, M'lord, watching us, watching town."

"How many?" snapped the prefect.

The witling's face twisted in concentration. "Hard to say. Two, I think . . . they have a little house there and they sit and watch us from inside. And they're strange. One's so big, so tall . . . much taller even than the honored Guildsman." He nodded at Thengets del Prou. ". . . I go close, closer, quiet like the paddlefoot, and then . . ."

His voice faded, as he stared beyond the thick stone walls at some remembered vision. Faintly, the prefect heard the wind keening through the twilight outside. He shivered. This place was so far north of where decent men should live. "Well?" he asked finally. "What happened then?"

"I run. I run! I'm so scared." The old man collapsed blubbering onto his stone chair.

Moragha turned on Lagha. "For this you waste my time, freeman? Don't you know that the prince-imperial"—*the witling, boorish prince-imperial*—"arrives in the Bodgaru prefecture tomorrow? I have more important things to do than listen to the ravings of your village idiot!"

Lagha's civility faded the tiniest fraction. "My Lord Prefect, Hugo has certain—problems, but he has been the property of my association for nearly thirty years, and in all that time I don't believe he has ever told tales." The object of their discussion sat looking dismally at the floor. "Frankly, My Lord, I believe he saw *something* up there."

"Squatters?" asked Prou.

"I don't know, sir. There are things that don't fit: the creatures are very strange, by Hugo's telling. That's why I thought My Lord Prefect might want to commission you to seng the hills. If there's a number of Snowfolk squatters up there you would detect it. And if these strange things be something else . . ." His voice trailed off.

Moragha wondered briefly why the bad luck always happened to him. The prince-imperial was an untalented lout, a stain upon the royal family's honor, but he *was* first in line of succession, and he *was* visiting the prefecture tomorrow. That visit was very important to Parapfu Moragha. But now there was this new problem to worry about; it just wasn't fair. On the other hand—and here the prefect brightened—in the unlikely event that there were Snowfolk close to town, his detecting them on the eve of the imperial visit would indeed be a coup. . . . Even if he had to deal with the Guild to achieve it.

"Well," he said grumpily to Thengets del Prou, "will you reconnoiter that area for us?"

Prou stretched his long legs lazily toward Moragha's throne. "You know the Guild doesn't like to involve itself with disputes between kingdoms."

"But we don't know for sure what it is Hugo saw up there," said Lagha.

"True," said the Guildsman. "Very well, My Lord Prefect, I will take the job. The Guild's commission will be one hundred imperials."

Moragha started. That was ten times the usual seng fee. "Go to it, then."

Prou nodded, closed his eyes, and seemed to relax even more. There was a long silence as the dark-faced young man senged far beyond the manse. Moragha closed his own eyes. He had always prided himself on his Talent. He could easily perceive the densities of the rock and air beyond the walls of the manse. His artisans had arranged the flagstones about the building in subtle patterns of varying density, and every part of that design was clear to him. Beyond that he could seng several transit pools in the area, but the spaces in between were hazy, and without visiting them personally he never could quite place them in true space. That was the only real difference between himself and the likes of Thengets del Prou, who even now was perceiving densities thousands of yards up in the hills. Moragha tried to imagine what it must be like to have such omniscience—but as always, he failed.

Finally the Guildsman opened his eyes. For a moment he seemed disoriented. Then, "You just wasted one hundred imperials, My Lord Perfect," he said. "I senged nothing up there but the densities of snow and rock."

There was something strange in the other's expression, and Moragha struggled for a moment to identify it. There was no laughter behind Prou's dark eyes! That was it. For the first time in the nearly two years he had known the man, that ironic glint was gone. The Guildsman had senged something, something so important he was willing to break the Guild's bond to lie about it. Moragha suppressed a sneer, and said, "Thank you, good Thengets, but I think I will check further. The Royal Atsobi Garrison is only one league to the south. I can have a company of mountain troops up here in an hour. Freeman Lagha, you'll have your Hugo direct the imperial soldiers. Any questions or comments?"

Moragha raised his hand in dismissal. Lagha retired with Hugo to the salt water pool at the center of the room and departed. The prefect stood as the Guildsman prepared to slip into the water after them. "A moment, good Thengets."

"Yes?" The Guildsman had recovered his old composure. There was even the beginning of a faint smile on his face.

"Are you sure you didn't miss anything on your survey?"

"Of course not, My Lord. You know it's nearly impossible to detect objects as small as individual men—their densities are so much like water. But there is no large group up there, I assure you."

"Very good. Still, it might be wise for you to stay in town the next few hours. If my troops were to find you up in the hills, we might conclude that you had senged something strange up there and were trying to get to it first. I would never want the Guild to be suspected of violating the trust we put in it."

Thengets del Prou stood very still for a moment, his smile slowly broadening. Finally he said, "As you wish, My Lord Prefect."

Two

Late in the afternoon, the archaeologist and the space pilot began packing their equipment. For twenty days, they had worked out of the bubble tent hidden among the peculiar three-crowned evergreens northeast of the alien village. They had probed that village with their telephoto cameras and their sensitive microphones. The archaeologist had recorded everything and talked to his computer, and now the space pilot thought they understood the language—

"Of course we understand the language, Bjault," said Yoninne Leg-Wot, the irritation showing sharply in her voice. She dropped the twenty-kilogram bulk of the collapsed tent onto the sledge and turned to glare at the spindly archaeologist. "I know, I know: There are 'subtleties we don't yet grasp.' The only people we've consistently been able to eavesdrop on are children and women. But we've got a good-sized vocabulary and a handle on the grammar. And with these new imprinting techniques, we won't forget them. Hell, I speak this Azhiri lingo better than English even though they made me take three years of that back at the Academy."

Ajão Bjault looked away from the stocky woman and tried not to grit his teeth. For the last twenty days he had had to live with her. With any other woman, such an extended companionship would have generated all sorts of scandalous rumors—even though Bjault was well into middle age, prolongevity treatments or no. But Yoninne Leg-Wot combined a squat, slablike body with a clever mind and a crippled personality. Among the crew, and probably the colonists as well, she would have been the hands-down winner of any unpopularity contest. And though Bjault understood her problems, and tried to be friendly, more and more he felt like a diffident fool.

"I don't know, Yoninne. It seems to me that some of the things we don't understand could be awfully important. There is a whole class of words—*reng, seng, keng, dgeng*—which are high-frequency but which we can't relate to their activities."

Leg-Wot shrugged, swept the last outstanding piece of equipment—a video recorder—into the sledge, and zipped the plastic cover shut over the cargo. She grabbed the control box and punched START. The sledge's oxyhydrogen fuel cells revived, the motors whined faintly, and the tiny sledge started up the hillside at a slow walking pace. To continue the conversation Bjault was forced to follow her.

"Futhermore, why have we seen so few men out-of-doors? What are the men doing? How do they make a living?"

"We've been over all this, Bjault. These guys are miners. They spend most of their time underground. These hills are lousy with copper. And I'll bet the '-*eng*' class words have to do with mining, so it's no wonder we haven't observed the activities they refer to."

"But how do they move the ore or its refinements out of here? The roads—" *Yes, the roads.* Before leaving orbit, Ajão had seen the photos Draere was taking. There were roads, but they were scarcely more than footpaths going from one lake to the next in the pattern of small, artificial lakes that netted the planet's inhabited continents. In some cases, those "roads" arced with geometrical precision across hundreds of kilometers—yet they did not follow great circles. It was Draere who pointed out that the curves they followed were the intersection of the planet's surface with planes parallel to its axis of rotation. How could the Azhiri race be capable of such precision and still be unaware that the shortest distance between two points on a sphere is a great circle?

Yoninne interrupted him impatiently. "Oh, *please*, Bjault. There may be some puzzling things about this civilization, but basically there is nothing to fear here. We know for certain that the Azhiri don't have atomics or electricity. From what we've seen they don't even have gunpowder. They live well enough, I suppose, but they're *primitive*.

"Where is your spirit of adventure? This is only the fifth time in thirteen thousand years that the human race has run across another intelligent species—or even the artifacts of another species. It would be a hell of a surprise to me if there *weren't* a lot of unanswered questions." She twisted a toggle on the control box and the sledge pivoted on its left track to avoid a large boulder. They followed, walking in the deep tread marks it left in the drifts. It was snowing, and the overcast made the twilight deeper than it would otherwise have been.

"Believe me, Yoninne, I am excited—though there's a good chance we've just stumbled on a lost colony. But I think we should wait, and look around some more before we call in the ferry. The expedition only has three ferries. If our situation goes sour I'm not sure that they'd divert another one from the colony on Novamerika."

"Well, fortunately, Draere didn't agree with you. When I messaged her, she seemed more than eager to get off that Godforsaken little island she's been stuck on the last few days. Cheer up. You'll have people to talk to besides me."

How true, thought Bjault. He turned up his heater and fell into step behind Leg-Wot. The wet snow was coming down thickly now, so thick that the village and the ocean were completely invisible. In the deep twilight, Leg-Wot and the sledge were little more than shadows. No trace of wind rustled the twisted evergreens around them. The only sounds were the *crunch-crunch* of the snow beneath their feet, the whine of the sledge's motors, and the faint—yet all-pervasive—hiss of the snow falling on the forest.

This heavy snowfall had been one reason Draere and her fellow officers had chosen tonight for landing. The locals wouldn't catch sight of the ferry's landing jets through this murk. In fact, the sound of the jets would be muted considerably by the snow-filled air. And since there was no wind, the ferry would have no trouble homing on the radio reflector he and Leg-Wot had set up in the valley seven kilometers north of town.

The darkness was almost complete now, but Yoninne Leg-Wot confidently guided the sledge toward the pass in the hills ahead. He had to admire the girl sometimes. Among other things, she had an uncanny sense of direction. If all the Novamerikan colony could spare for this ground reconnaissance were a couple of social rejects, then they could have done worse than send Yoninne Leg-Wot and the senile archaeologist Ajão Bjault. *Let's not be maudlin*, Ajão told himself. *At your age you could never have wangled a colonist's berth without the respect of a lot of people. You were lucky beyond all justice that this solar system has two habitable planets. And then an intelligent species is discovered on one of them, and you still whine about your declining career!*

He shook the snow from his head and pulled the hood down over his face. There was something vastly peaceful about a thick, quiet snowfall. Except for the ever-present drag of this world's higher gravity, he could almost imagine that he was back on Homeworld, three parsecs—and forty years—away.

Leg-Wot fell back so that they walked abreast. "I think we're being followed," she said softly.

"What!" His response was halfway between a hiss and a scream.

"Yeah. Take this," she handed him the sledge's control box, "and gimme the maser. Okay, now let's keep walking. I think there's only one, and he's keeping his distance."

Bjault did not dispute the instructions. He tried to see into the deepening gray. It was no use. It was hard enough to see a pine tree just ahead in time to walk the sledge around it. Yoninne must have heard something; her ears were much more acute than his.

On his right Leg-Wot fumbled about as she checked the maser, then pointed it into the sky to the north. She spoke the appropriate call signs into her hood mike, but there was no response. That wasn't too surprising. In order to save fuel, the ferry was making an unpowered entry, using the planet's atmosphere to slow itself down. No doubt the spacecraft was momentarily blacked out by entry ionization.

Leg-Wot waited two minutes, then repeated her call. Almost immediately, Bjault's earphone came alive with Draere's cheerful voice. "Hello, down there!" the voice said, ignoring standard radio procedure. "We're about sixty kilometers up and coming down fast. Never fear, the mail will arrive on time."

Leg-Wot outlined their situation to the descending ferry. "Okay," came Draere's voice, "I understand. If you can hold on for another ten minutes, you'll be all right, I think. The ferry's landing jets are guaranteed to scare the wits out of the uninitiated, and if that doesn't work, we do have some firepower aboard—Holmgre and his entire platoon. We didn't leave anything but some robot radios on that miserable little island.

"Keep in touch. You should be able to switch to your omnies any minute now."

"Wilco, out," Leg-Wot replied. They had reached the pass in the ridge line and were starting down the other side. Here the snow lay much deeper, the product of more than one storm. The sledge churned along just ahead of them, its treads acting as tiny paddles in the loose snow. The woman retrieved the sledge control from Bjault and guided them down the slope toward their ablation skiff.

Still he heard nothing but their own footsteps and the sound of the sledge. Perhaps Yoninne had heard some large animal. He loosened his machine pistol in its holster. They knew there were such things: their sonic fence had scared away something big just the day before.

Leg-Wot turned the sledge hard right, let it run on about two meters, then halted it. It was completely dark now. As Ajão walked forward he nearly tripped over a curving mound covered with a few centimeters of fluff snow. The ablation skiff! Bjault went to one knee and swept the snow from its hull. There was something comforting about the feel of the scorched ceramic beneath his gloves, even though the skiff would never fly again. The ablation skiff was nothing more than a spherical hulk, three meters across. Inside there was barely enough room for two humans, their equipment, and the skiff's parachute. The little craft had no power of its own, and there was really only one mission it could ever fly: dropped from an orbiting spacecraft, it burned its way down through the upper atmosphere to an altitude and a speed where the parachute could bring it to a gentle landing. In concept the ablation skiff was nearly as old—and as simple—as the wheel. No doubt the human race had rediscovered both dozens of times during the last thirteen thousand years.

Yoninne's voice came softly into his ear. Apparently she had sealed her suit and was speaking—whispering—to him over the hood radio. "Let's stick to radios from now on, Bjault. I drove the sledge off to one side, so whoever-it-is that's following us may get the wrong idea. I'm crawling back to the skiff now. If we just lie quiet in the snow, I don't see how they can know exactly where we are—just remember, we're the guys with the automatic weapons."

Ajão closed his hood. "Yes," he whispered back, though he wasn't sure if he could bring himself to play mass executioner, even in a pinch.

He relaxed in the snow, listened. The hood's earphone had a good acoustical link with the outside air, but he heard nothing beyond that faint hiss of endlessly falling snow. Somewhere to the north, way, way out in the dark—perhaps ten kilometers up, still—the ferry was plummeting toward them at hundreds of meters per second. Five hundred tons of titanium and plastic just—falling. When would Draere kick on her landing jets?

As if in answer to his thoughts, Draere's voice sounded in Bjault's ear. "Any trouble with the locals?"

"No, but Yoninne thinks we still have some undesired company."

"Aha." Pause. "Well, I just lit my jets. I wonder what they'll make of that. See you."

The silence stretched on for another thirty seconds. Then a vast and continuous rumble swept over them. The ferry was still so far away that all but the lowest frequencies were smeared out by the air. What was left sounded like strange thunder; it started loud, and just kept getting louder and louder. To anyone not acquainted with reaction motors it must have sounded like an immense monster, only a few hundred meters away and coming closer.

A pearly white light glowed faintly in the blackness above and to the north of them: even the light from plasma jets had trouble penetrating the thousands of meters of thickly falling snow. Through the mike he could hear Draere calmly reading out the ferry's altitude.

Louder, louder, the sound came till it was a physical force pushing at him through both air and ground. Winds generated by the superheated air from the jets whirled the snow up and around him. The very storm itself was being shattered by the energy these jets were pumping into it. Ajão tried to bury his faceplate in the snow, but out of the corner of his eye he could see the needlelike blue flames of the ferry's three plasma jets. *A perfectly normal night landing,* he chuckled to himself, and tried to burrow deeper into the snow. God, it was going to be wonderful to have a shower and some decent food. Most of all, wonderful to get away from Yoninne Leg-Wot.

Draere's voice came distorted and faint against the roar,

"Three hundred meters up, and your reflector is shining loud and clear directly under us. Hold on, gang."

The ferry's thirty-meter bulk hovered, then slowly descended on the reflector Bjault and Leg-Wot had set at the bottom of the valley, three thousand meters away. The snowstorm was literally blown away from around it, and looking up, Bjault could see the hillsides lit by painfully bright, electric-blue light. Ajão gasped. They *had* been followed: across the blue-lit snowfields, dozens of figures stood silhouetted in the glare.

But the ferry was less than fifty meters up now, and—the craft lurched slightly, then toppled to one side. Draere's voice came as calmly as if she were discussing ancient history. "Ground turbulence like I've never seen." Two of the ferry's jets brightened and the craft shot off to the side, slowly gaining altitude. "I can't recover . . ."

The blunt-nosed ferry curved gracefully downward, smashed sideways into the valley floor, and exploded in flashes of blue-white flame as the jets' plasma escaped confinement.

Bjault's jaw went slack. Draere, forty people, all dead . . . in less than a second. He lay dazed for a moment as gobs of flaming wreckage rained down out of the sky. Around the crash site there were only chemical fires now—ugly red and orange flames that were virtually silent compared to the plasma jets.

The ringing in his ears subsided and he heard voices. Bjault tilted his head to look across the snow at the sledge. There stood three natives. The orange firelight flickered across them and the turtlelike form of the sledge, as a light breeze brought the snowfall back over the hillside. Ajão squinted at the trio. They could have been the fellows he had seen during the landing, but if so they had moved awfully fast in those last instants before Draere and the others crashed. The men appeared to be normal Azhiri: squat-bodied and light-skinned. They were dressed in gray-and-white camouflage uniforms that Bjault associated with automatic-weapons warfare; soldiers from more primitive cultures usually dressed like peacocks or else went about in ragged civilian clothes. But the only weapons Bjault could see on the men were machetes strapped securely to their sides.

Bjault kept absolutely still. The snow was falling faster now. Perhaps he and Leg-Wot could yet evade capture—though what good would that be? They were truly ship-wrecked now. He concentrated on the others' fast, slurred speech. "A little monster, like that huge one perhaps," one of them said, and kicked at the sledge's treads, "but at least it is dead. Apfaneru, this is bvepfesh. . . ." His voice trailed into frightened silence.

"Ahe, look!" The second soldier grabbed the first's arm and pointed off to Ajāo's right. "You there! On your life—don't move!"

The three started off in the direction the soldier had pointed. Suddenly the dormant sledge surged forward, its electric motors whining at full power. Apparently Leg-Wot still had control of it. "The monster!" screamed the third soldier as the sledge bowled him over. The second Azhiri whirled upon the machine, and a thunderlike snapping sound shook the ground. The snow whirled up around the sledge, and when it cleared, he saw the vehicle was on its side, and on fire.

Now things were moving too fast for Bjault to follow. On his right, Leg-Wot had risen to her knees, her machine-pistol covering the three Azhiri. Again that massive snapping sound. The snow blew up around her, and she was thrown head over heels into the drift behind her.

Suddenly the first soldier was beside her. "Ho! So that's why you didn't try to escape." He seemed relaxed now, almost jovial. "You are a witling." Ajão raised his head slightly. The snow was coming down as heavily as before the landing, but by the guttering fires he glimpsed several other troopers in the near distance. The men were systematically searching the snowfield. Each trooper kept five meters between himself and the next man—just like modern soldiers wary of automatic weapons fire. *Why, why?*

Heavy hands grabbed him under the armpits. "We have found another, Dgedga," shouted his captor. "A witling also." His pistol was taken and he was half-carried, half-dragged past the sledge toward Leg-Wot. The soldier dropped Bjault beside the girl and disappeared into the snowstorm. It was almost humiliating how casually they were left here, apparently unguarded. The darkness had returned, but Ajão heard the soldiers moving back and forth across the hillside, probing the snow. In minutes the Azhiri discovered the ablation skiff and its fiberene parachute.

The one called Apfaneru spoke loudly, "Group four will remain here through the night. Be alert. There may be more monsters. Group leaders may call for help at the smallest sign. Groups two and three will take what remains of the monsters. Group one: the witlings go to the deepest dungeon in Deleru Moragha."

Again Ajão was picked up and dragged through the snow. Behind him he could tell that Leg-Wot was getting the same treatment. How badly had Yoninne been hurt? Was she unconscious, or worse?

They stopped and Bjault got to his feet. He saw what looked like a steel pot, perhaps two meters in diameter. It was suspended from a heavy timber tripod, and beneath the pot, a trooper was trying to keep some kindling afire. With a sudden shiver of fear, Ajão guessed that the pot was filled with water. He struggled frantically back from his captor, but the other man was built for this gravity, and Ajão was slapped to the ground. "Witling, if you don't wish to be hurt you will climb in." Then the soldier piled a further incredibility on the scene: he turned and climbed the narrow wooden ladder that led over the flames to the lip of the pot. There was a loud splash as he jumped in.

Bjault stared blankly for a moment. Someone pushed him roughly from behind. "You heard the man, witling. Move!" He stepped forward and awkwardly climbed the closely spaced rungs. Behind him another soldier dragged the now weakly struggling Leg-Wot up the ladder. Ajão stopped at the lip of the pot and looked down, for a moment saw nothing. Then he heard the voice of the fellow who had jumped in. "*Iou*, this water's cold. Should have waited till they had the fire going properly." The native was holding onto the lip so that just his head was out of the water. "Jump in, you two. The quicker in, the quicker out."

Bjault tried to ease himself over the edge, but the snow along the lip was slippery and he splashed awkwardly into the water. Lord, it *was* cold. He couldn't take more than three or four minutes of this without his heated suit. He kicked himself to the surface just in time to be smashed downward again by Leg-Wot. They bobbed to the surface, the woman swearing loudly. *She's all right, then!* Ajão thought with relief. He trod water frantically, trying to find a hand hold, but the soldier grabbed his shoulder. "Where are you from anyway, witling? Let yourselves sink below the surface." They did as they were told. Ajão was at the point now that things seemed more like dream than reality.

He looked up through the water. The darkness was not complete. Something strangely green, quite unlike torchlight, glowed above them. Then strong hands pushed against his buttocks and he and Yoninne burst through the surface. Gasping, they pulled themselves from the water, assisted by the soldier below. Bjault lay back dazedly on the warm stone floor. The air stank of human waste and worse. He saw now that they were in a featureless chamber some three meters across. The green glow came from phosphorescent fungus that hung in great loops from the raw bedrock of the walls. He could see no doors, no ventilation holes.

The trooper bobbed through the green glinting surface of the water, his pale face asmile. "Comfortable?" He gestured at the dark stone that surrounded them on all sides. "It would take a Guildsman to get out of this thing, so I don't think the prefect has to worry about a pair of witlings escaping." He let go of the edge and slipped below the surface. Yoninne rose painfully to her knees and crawled to the edge of the pool. Ajão followed her, and they looked into the water. The light from above was faint, but he could see the bottom. There was no sign of the trooper. He dipped his hand into the scummy water.

Leg-Wot stared and stared down into the pool. "Teleports. They're goddamned teleports," she said finally.

Three

The Bodgaru terminus of the Royal Road had been carefully prepared for the prince-imperial's arrival. Except for an army escort boat, which had arrived minutes before, the lake was free of traffic. All along the water's edge, the season's first ice had been chipped away and the stonework polished. Many ninedays before, the prefect had imported an ornamental jade garden and "planted" it along the wharf side of the lake. The life-sized stone trees and shrubs were adorned with hundreds of flowers carved from yellow and blue topaz. That morning the townsmen had dusted every trace of snow from the jade garden, so that now it sparkled with sterile grace.

The townspeople stood all along the wharf. Every man, woman, and child held tiny replicas of the imperial tricolor, issued them by the prefect's men. Their talk was cheerful and unrestrained. Though their attendance was required, most waited eagerly: The visit of a member of the royal-imperial family was a rare event. No one realized this more clearly, more agonizingly, than the prefect himself. Parapfu Moragha stood at stiff attention, between the garrison band and his jade garden.

Though the sun hung at noon in the deep blue sky, the wind blowing across the lake was chilling, and the snow-covered, pine-covered hills that rose above the lake made it seem a frigid blue puddle caught at the edge of winter.

Suddenly the quiet surface of the lake was no longer empty. The royal yacht popped into existence, slamming down and eastward through the water. The white hull almost disappeared beneath the surface, then bobbed back up, its timbers creaking. Two-foot waves rippled back and forth across the lake, splashed icy water along the wharf. Even before the yacht had stopped rocking, its crew ran out the imperial tricolor: the yellow sun in a sky of blue over a field of green. The band on the shore struck up a cheery welcome as the road boat edged toward shore.

On the yacht's private deck, Pelio-nge-Shozheru, prince-imperial of All Summer, undid his safety harness and got up to walk to the railing. Though taller than the average Azhiri, Pelio wasn't much more than a boy. He wore a green-and-blue kilt with his rank woven across the waist, but even without the costume, his wide nose and green eyes would have at least identified him as one of the nobility. One would never guess that the prince was a witling, so devoid of Talent that his kenging could scarcely kill a sandmite.

A warm summer breeze, renged from the southern hemisphere—as far south of the equator as Bodgaru was north—blew softly across the deck to warm Pelio's back and insulate him from the local chill. The servants who cast those breezes sat below decks, as did the lords and ladies accompanying him. The prince stood alone, or as alone as he could ever be: only his bodyguards and his watchbear were with him on the deck. That was more protection than the average noble felt obliged to keep—but Pelio was a witling, and without his guards' constant attention, the lowliest peasant could scramble his innards.

Pelio looked across the water at the cheering crowds and the garrison band. *I wonder if they are laughing inside*, he thought, *while they cheer with their mouths.* That a witling should one day be king-imperial was indeed a great joke. No doubt several of the rustics in that crowd *owned* unfortunates possessing more Talent than he. That was the normal fate of witlings. They were defenseless against every teleportive jape of normal people. A witling was treated as a chattel—unless, of course, he was born into the royal family, unless he was heir apparent to an empire. Pelio's eyes stung with the old shame as he looked past the hundreds of townspeople waving their little tricolors: how wonderful his birth must have seemed to the Summerkingdom! For years his father had been childless, the dynasty imperiled—and then at last, at the very end of his father's middle age, a fertile consort had been found. Pelio often imagined how his father must have suffered as it became apparant that his son was not superior, not normal, not even retarded—that his son would never display more than the smallest bit of Talent. And to top tragedy with insult, just one year later, Pelio's mother, Consort Queen Virizhiana, gave birth to Aleru. But for a matter of dates, Prince Aleru would be first in line—and Aleru was perfectly normal, with more than average Talent.

Naturally, Pelio's position in the royal court was an embarrassment. King Shozheru lacked the harshness of will to execute his firstborn—and such execution was the only accepted method of clearing the line of succession for the secondborn. It was not surprising that the closest things Pelio

had to friends at court were the obsequious intriguers who lied to and flattered him; the closest thing to respect, the honest hatred of his brother and his mother.

Every few seasons, protocol dictated that Pelio take his yacht and visit some corner of the kingdom. Often such tours exposed him to less skillfully disguised derision than he faced at the Summerpalace, but at least the faces were different. Besides, the Summerkingdom was such a vast and beautiful place, it almost made him forget himself and his weaknesses. And sometimes the trips were not as tame as the royal advisers would like. Perhaps this would be one of those times. The strange message he had received that morning was anonymous, yet explicit: there had been a skirmish at Bodgaru with monsters or Snowfolk. . . .

The troopers ashore gathered in the tow ropes and pulled the barge toward the timbers that cushioned the wharf. The prefect and the garrison band were almost directly below him now. He smiled slightly as he saw Moragha start. The prefect must have felt the warm wind blowing off the yacht.

The boat bounced gently against the timbers and the soldiers made her fast. Pelio saluted the crowd and turned away from the railing. "Here, Samadhom," he called softly to his watchbear. The sand-colored beast padded over to him and began licking his hand. The prince trusted his watchbear more than any of his guards—and as a passive defense against keng attack, the shaggy animal was probably as effective as any Azhiri, Guildsmen excepted. Pelio patted Samadhom's head, and then, together with his silent guards, he descended the stairway to the first deck. The lords and ladies who joined them at the second deck were not so quiet, but Pelio did not respond to their eternal, artificial good cheer. With his entourage close behind, he crossed the filigreed iron drop-bridge to the wharf, and walked to where Parapfu Moragha stood at backbreaking attention.

"You may rest, good Parapfu."

Moragha relaxed with visible relief and signaled the garrison band to sound Rest. Across the wharf, the townsfolk broke the silence they had kept since the Prince set foot on land.

"Your Highness, the people of my prefecture—myself included—welcome your visit with the greatest love and respect." Moragha's head bobbed with enthusiasm. The prefect turned and waved Pelio up the inlaid steps that led to the prefectural manse. "There are so many things we have to show Your Royal-Imperial Highness." Moragha dropped into step just behind Pelio, cutting between the prince and his retinue. "Bodgaru is the northernmost reach of Summer, yet we maintain the spirit of green growing things in our hearts and works." He waved at the jade garden that stood on both sides of their path. Pelio followed his gesture but did not comment. He saw that the green and yellow stones were cleverly carved, and he could dimly seng that the density patterns of the stonework resembled those of real plants. But there was a touch of gaucherie in imitating life with stone or snow. It was the sort of thing he had seen taken to an abstracted extreme in the Snowking's crystal palace at the ends of the world. "And," Moragha rushed on when he got no response, "the mining caves of Bodgaru are the largest in the world. Summerfolk have mined the copper hereabouts for more than a century. . . ."

From the rear of the party, servants continued to teleport a warm breeze in from the southern hemisphere. Beside Pelio, the prefect was beginning to sweat in his tooled leather oversuit, but the warm air had less to do with that than the prince's continued silence. Few flatterers could contend with his stony silence and expressionless gaze. At court, his silence was regarded as a sign of boorishness, stupidity. And in truth, there was arrogance in Pelio's manner—but there was more distrust and loneliness.

Finally Moragha's prepared speech ground to a halt. The two walked silently for many paces, until Pelio looked at the other, and said, "Tell me about last night's skirmish, good Parapfu."

"How did you—" the prefect started, then gargled back his surprise. "There is not a great deal to tell, Your Highness. The affair is still a mystery. My agents detected intruders in the hills to the north. I dispatched troops from the garrison. They encountered a large flying creature, which they destroyed."

"And the intruders?" prodded the boy.

The prefect waved his hand in casual dismissal. "Witl—persons of no account, Your Highness."

Witlings! So his anonymous informant had written the truth. Imagine witlings fighting normal people. "Snowfolk?" Pelio asked casually, trying to hide his excitement.

"No, Your Highness. At least, I have never seen any Snowmen like them."

"I will interview them."

"But Baron-General Ngatheru has expert interrogators at Atsobi. . . ."

You self-contradicting fool, thought Pelio. *So you have something really interesting here.*

"The strangers have been moved to the garrison?"

"Uh, no, Your Highness, they are in one of the dungeons beneath my manse. The baron-general thought—"

"Fine, Parapfu. Then I will interview these strange prisoners immediately."

The prefect knew better than to oppose a royal whim, even Pelio's. "Certainly, Your Highness. It will be most convenient to use the transit pool in my manse."

By now they had reached the rose-quartz terrace surrounding the prefect's home. The manse was only five hundred feet from the lake, but it was some fifty feet up the side of the ridge line that protected the Royal Road's terminus against surveillance from the north. No wonder Moragha had not suggested they teleport to the manse: using a transit pool in weather like this would be a cold and unpleasant business.

Like most buildings in wintry regions, the manse had a doorway carved through its walls. Pelio liked doorways; they gave him some of the mobility other people had naturally. Inside the manse there was too little space for Pelio's wind rengers to do their job, and the rooms were chill and stale. The pale light filtering through the windows was a good deal less cheerful than what Pelio was used to in the open ballrooms of the Summerpalace. Moragha's bondsmen circulated among the nobles with drink and candy. The prefect had even managed to import a small group of singers from south of Atsobi. It was a festive scene . . . of sorts.

Parapfu led the prince and his guards away from the crowd and through a wilted interior garden to the manse's transit pool, where his servants produced watertight slickers.

"The dungeon is nearly sixteen hundred feet below ground level, Your Highness, so I deem the transit pool the most convenient entrance."

Pelio nodded, slipped into the slicker. If Moragha were sufficiently skilled, they could jump right from where they were standing. But sixteen hundred feet was a long way down. Once he had been jumped two thousand feet downward—directly, without first submerging in a transit pool. The heat shock had given him a headache that lasted a nineday.

The water in the pool was cold and oily. Pelio was grateful for the watertight suit, even if it was an awkward nuisance.

(It just proved again that the only sensible place for people to live was in the tropics, where winter never came.) In the water around him, Pelio could seng a familiar tension as Moragha prepared to jump. A second passed. The tension "brightened," then twisted in upon itself as the pool and its contents were exchanged with the destination pool.

They bobbed to the surface, the guards immediately taking positions around the pool. Pelio and Moragha pulled themselves from the water. The air stank, and the rockwort on the walls glowed bright green: the air hadn't been changed for many hours. The green-lit dungeon was large, and fairly warm—yet it was still nothing more than an empty space carved from abyssal bedrock. Without the constant attention of the keepers who knew its location the cell would quickly become a coffin for its prisoners.

"All right, on your feet," came Moragha's sharp voice. His man began kicking at the dark-clothed shapes on the floor. Pelio suppressed a gasp as the first of the strangers stood. The man—creature?—was incredibly tall, well over six feet. But even more grotesque was the spindly thinness of his limbs. The fellow looked as though he would shatter if he ever took a bad fall.

"I *said* get up. Come to attention. You have been accorded an undeserved honor. Get *up!*" Moragha aimed a kick at the second creature, who rolled lithely to its feet as if it had been watching them alertly all the while.

To Pelio, the rest of the universe retreated to a position of total irrelevance. He didn't hear the stifled gasps of the guards. He didn't notice the silence that stretched on and on.

She was *beautiful*. The girl stood tall, as tall as Pelio, yet slender as a woods-doe. Even in the dim light her coveralls revealed the strange perfection of her figure. And her face—its beauty was unworldly. Her features were sharp, her nose and chin almost pointed. It was as if the dark, grotesque face of the tall one had been treated by a kinder artist. While the skin of the Snowfolk was chalky white, and Pelio's was grayish green, her skin was almost black in the rockwort's light. Her smooth face might have been carved from darkwood. All the childhood fairy tales of woods-elves and dryads came rushing to mind. She was the stuff of dreams.

Pelio spent an unmeasured time lost in the deep, dark eyes that stared from that miraculous face. Finally the spell weakened and he asked faintly, "And she . . . they are witlings, Parapfu?"

"As I said, Your Highness," the prefect replied, looking at Pelio strangely.

"Do they speak Azhiri?"

"At least a little."

Pelio turned back to the girl, and spoke slowly, "What is your name?"

"Yoninne." Her answer was clear, but with overtones of fear and tension.

"Ionina? A strange name. Where are you come from, Ionina?"

"From—" Her answer was interrupted by an abrupt though unintelligible command from the spindly giant. The girl replied in kind, then turned back to Pelio. "No, I no tell that." She backed away from them, looking both defiant and brave. . . . *And she a witling*, thought Pelio.

Then he made his decision, and tried not to think of what might happen when his father heard of it. "Prefect, you have done well to detect and capture these intruders; I commend you. They seem interesting indeed. I will take them with me on my return to the Summerpalace."

"Your Highness! These are dangerous people. The monsters that accompanied them were so loud that we could hear them even here in Bodgaru."

Pelio turned on the prefect, and his smile was full of vengeance. "Dangerous, you say, good Parapfu? And they witlings? How *could* they be dangerous? Did they harm Ngatheru's troops?"

"No, Your Highness," admitted Moragha, the barest hint of sullenness creeping into his voice. "In fact, if they had attempted any attack on the troops, they almost certainly would be dead now. But sir, it is not their persons that are so dangerous. Baron-General Ngatheru is convinced that they can explain the monster fragments that were left after the battle."

"Fine. I will take whatever of those fragments you have. Don't interrupt. If my cousin Ngatheru is still upset with the situation, let him take it up with me or my father," he said, praying that Ngatheru would decide to let the matter drop. After all, the baron-general was five tiers below Pelio as formal nobility was counted.

"Yes, Your Highness." The prefect came briefly to attention as he capitulated.

Pelio took a last look into the dryad's dark, mysterious eyes, then turned to slip into the transit pool. *She is the most beautiful creature . . .*

. . . And, like me, a witling.

Four

"M e? Play up to that flat-noised, gray-faced savage? I'd rather die." Yoninne Leg-Wot crossed her thick, muscular arms and glared at Bjault.

Ajão leaned toward the irate pilot as far as the leather restraints would permit. "Look, Yoninne, I'm not asking you to, to do anything immoral. I'm just saying that this fellow likes you—and he's obviously very powerful. If his title," and here he pronounced an Azhiri phrase, "means what I think, then he is the number-one or number-two man in their state, even as young as he seems. We need his goodwill."

For a long moment Leg-Wot scowled down at the boat's polished deck. Bjault suddenly wondered if she were really so disgusted at the thought of getting friendly with the young Azhiri, or if she were just so twisted by past romantic failures that she couldn't even playact anymore.

It wasn't until this Pelio had talked to them that Ajão realized how much Leg-Wot looked like an Azhiri. She was a little tall, perhaps, but she had the build and the hardness—if not the coloring—of the aliens. Of course there were many differences: the Azhiri bone and cartilage structure was vastly different. Their features looked as though they had been pressed from soft clay, then smoothed until nose, chin, brow, and ears were all rounded and indistinct. Pelio was either very spoiled or very lonely to take to someone who must look as exotically strange as Leg-Wot.

But this was exactly the sort of good fortune they needed now. Less than an hour after Pelio left the dungeon, Bjault and Leg-Wot had been teleported (what other word could he use?) to a clean, comfortable cell, where they were treated to warm baths and a meal. The next morning, they had been led to a small lake—to board the strange round boat that floated there. Now Bjault guessed the solution to several of the mysteries that had confronted them before their capture. And if Pelio were really taking them elsewhere—as he had said in the dungeon— then that guess would be put to the test in just a few minutes.

Finally the woman answered him. "I don't see that it really matters, Bjault. You say that sucking up to this fellow is the only chance we have for survival. I say that it's just the difference between dying slow and dying fast. You yourself told me the local plants are tainted with heavy metals. I suppose we can still eat them, but we'll eventually be poisoned—no matter how chummy I get with this big shot. Our only hope is for rescue, but the suit radios are so damn weak, and this planet's ionosphere is so active, that any signal we send would get smeared unrecognizable. And even if Novamerika knew we were alive, it would be a stupid gamble for them to risk another ferry trying to pull us out of here." She lay back limply. Her old spirit seemed completely quenched.

It's almost as though she's making excuses, thought Bjault, *as if she'd rather not be rescued*. "You may not care whether 'the dying is slow or fast,' Yoninne, but the distinction is important to me, and perhaps to the whole human race. From what Pelio said, I think he's got part of our equipment: the ablation skiff, the pistols . . . and the maser. With the maser we *could* make ourselves heard on Novamerika; they must be listening to the telemetry station Draere set up. And as for the 'risk' they'd be taking to rescue us: don't you realize what we've stumbled into? This world could be the greatest find anyone has made since mankind left Old Earth—the greatest discovery in thirteen-thousand years. These Azhiri can *teleport*. Even if their trick doesn't violate relativity, even if they can't 'jump' faster than light, it still means that the entire structure of human colonization is going to be transformed. All down the centuries, man's colonies have been isolated by an abyss of time and space, and by the enormous cost of travel from one solar system to another. Colonial civilizations, as on Homeworld, rise and fall just as surely and just as rapidly as they did on Old Earth. No doubt man has colonized several thousand worlds, but we know of only a few hundred, and most of those through hearsay. Whatever greatness a civilization achieves dies with it, simply because we are so isolated."

Ajão realized his voice was gradually rising. He was making a point that haunted many, including Leg-Wot. How often and how loudly had he heard the pilot denounce the Homeworld Union for not spending more money on interstellar colonization, "trade," and radio searches for unknown civilizations. "But *now*," he continued, more softly, "we may have found a way around all this. If we can find the secret of the Azhiri Talent—even if we can alert Novamerika and eventually Homeworld to its existence—then the distances between the stars will not matter, and there could be a truly interstellar civilization."

Leg-Wot looked thoughtful, less glum. Bjault had always believed that humanity as a whole was one of the few things she really cared about. "I see what you mean. We've got to get back word, whether we survive or not. And we've got to learn everything we can about these people." Her face lit with sudden, unthinking enthusiasm. "Why do they always teleport from one pool of water to another? I'll bet these guys have a high-class technology hidden beneath all the medieval window dressing. The pools are some sort of transmitting devices."

Ajão breathed an inward sigh of relief that the girl had snapped out of her mood. It was hard enough dealing with his own discouragement. He shook his head, and said, "I think these people are every bit as backward as we thought before, Yoninne. I'll wager that teleportation is a natural mental ability with them."

"Well, then, why *do* they always seem to teleport from pools of water?"

Bjault's reply was lost in the shrill whistle that suddenly sounded from one of the boat's upper decks. It was almost like a steam whistle, though Ajão couldn't see where the sound came from. Whatever its origin, the whistle obviously signaled something important. The two guards who a moment before had been playing a dice game—at least it looked like dice, even though the stones were dodecahedra—stood up abruptly. One of them swept the dice into a leather bag. They both settled back in padded couches and strapped themselves in. The moment Ajão had seen all those couches, with their uniform system of restraints, he had guessed that they were only incidentally used to tie down prisoners. It was just one more bit of evidence for his theory. In another few moments he hoped to see a much more important confirmation.

The whistle continued to wail for nearly a minute, as crewmen and soldiers took their places. When the tone abruptly ended, he could hear the townspeople cheering on the pier somewhere behind him. They had dutifully assembled (or been assembled) to see their ruler off. It fit the cultural picture he had of this Azhiri state.

Bjault twisted around on his couch, trying to take in every detail. This boat was the strangest vehicle he had seen in all his 193 years. In basic form it was an oblate spheroid. The hull at least followed this description perfectly, while the three-tiered deck structure only approximately filled the outline of a spheroid. The craft sat low in the water, and its construction seemed much stronger than the planet's gravity required. Heavy wooden beams and thick planking were used everywhere. And though the craft was rich with ornamentation—paintings, tapestries, precious-metal inlays— there was no grillwork, and no overhanging ornaments. There was also no visible means of propulsion: no masts, no oarlocks.

Ajão found himself gathering all this in with a speed and interest he had not felt since . . . since he finished his exhumation of the library ruins at Ajeuribad, back on Homeworld more than a century before. His reconstruction of relativity theory from the charred microfilm records had eventually put Homeworld back in touch with the stars, after the two-thousand-year-long Interregnum. *But what we've discovered here could be yet more important*, thought Ajão. He almost felt young again.

The crewmen and guards around them seemed to tense. Whatever it was, it would happen any second now, though Ajão sensed nothing himself. He looked at Leg-Wot and she shook her head uncertainly. He glanced across the water at the shoreline two hundred meters to the east. The land beyond was rugged. The triple crown of the bluish green pines were lightly dusted by snow.

There was no flicker: the landscape simply vanished, was replaced by another much greener, much darker. Simultaneously his ears popped and the bottom dropped out of his stomach. Then the boat smashed back into the water and his couch rammed against his back. Around them the lake waters rose in a massive ring wall. Through the sounds of shattered water he heard the boat's timbers groan as they absorbed the sudden acceleration.

And the boat sat bobbing in the lake—a lake, anyway. It certainly wasn't the one they had been in a moment before.

The sky was dark, the air warm and wet. At first he thought it was night, but as his eyes adjusted, he realized that this was a normal overcast day. As the sounds of their arrival died, he heard the rain cascading past them along the boat's curving hull, falling upon the lake to make myriad transient craters in the water.

Boats flickered in and out of existence across that surface, sending good-sized waves splashing this way and that. Along the water's edge, camouflaged craft—military boats?—were arranged in neat rows, like pleasure boats in some Homeworld marina. Inland—obscured by the rain and trees—there was a collection of low, squat buildings with slit windows, all very reminiscent of field fortifications used back on Homeworld toward the end of the Interregnum: again, evidence that the Azhiri possessed some analog of automatic weapons and artillery. Somehow he had to fit that evidence with the rest of his theory.

Ajão turned to Leg-Wot, who had recovered from their abrupt arrival and the transformed landscape much faster than he. "You felt that jolt when we arrived, Yoninne? That's one good reason why these folks prefer to teleport out of water."

Leg-Wot's eyes widened in understanding. "The planet's rotational speed."

Ajão nodded. "At first glance teleportation seems like a simple—if supernormal—trick: you disappear at one point and appear at another, without ever suffering the inconvenience of having been in between. But closer inspection shows that nature imposes certain restrictions on even the supernormal. If you are moving relative to your destination, then there is naturally going to be a collison when you arrive—and the faster you're going, the harder the crash. This world rotates once every twenty-five hours, so points along the equator move eastward at better than five hundred meters per second, while points north and south rotate at correspondingly slower speeds. Teleporting across the planet's surface is like—"

"—Like playing hopscotch on a merry-go-round," said Yoninne. "And so they jump into water to cushion the impact of their arrival. Ha! I bet that accounts for those lake chains we saw from orbit: these people have to teleport in short jumps from puddle to puddle." Ajão nodded. Even with water to cushion the impact, these boats would be shattered if they splashed into their destination at more than a few meters per second. So they could not safely teleport more than a few hundred kilometers at a stroke. No, that wasn't quite right: from a given point in the northern hemisphere, you could teleport due south to the point whose south latitude was the same as your north latitude (and vice versa), since such pairs of points have the same velocity. But that was a quibble. Most long distance trips would require many jumps—and therefore strings of many transport lakes.

"But," continued Leg-Wot, "we should have seen this from orbit. We had plenty of pictures of these lakes and the boats in them. If those jackasses back on Novamerika had only spared us some decent reconnaissance equipment, we could have had continuous coverage of our ground track, and we would have seen these guys teleport. Hell, if Draere's people hadn't been so anxious to set up that telemetry station landside, they might have stayed in orbit long enough to—"

She was interrupted by the boat's warning whistle. Ajão wondered just how that sound was generated. *Jump.* Again he felt the sinking sensation as the boat rose westward from the surface of their destination lake, then smashed back into the water. It was raining here just as heavily as before, but they had definitely moved: this new lake was huge, and he could see dozens of other boats bulking darkly through the gloom. Long wooden buildings crowded the shoreline. Warehouses? Along the water's edge, work crews in slickers tied boats into the piers. The scene was busy, but there weren't as many laborers as Bjault would have expected in a medieval harbor. It was more like a jet- or a spaceport, where a few technicians loaded thousands of tons of cargo with automatic equipment. Then Ajão saw the reason for the seeming anachronism. Of course! The Azhiri workers could simply teleport cargo from their storehouses to the boats' holds, and vice versa. Probably the only real hand work was in the maintenance of the boats and buildings.

Again the whistle, and again they teleported. Ajão tried to keep track of each jump, but it was difficult. Not all lakes were set amidst fortifications and warehouses. Some were surrounded by deciduous forests whose fallen, three-pointed leaves turned the ground and the water's edge to orange and red and chartreuse. Jump followed jump, and the landscapes beyond their boat flickered swiftly by. As the minutes passed the air became almost tropically warm. The rainstorm was far behind them now. Sunlight streamed down through blue sky between blocky chunks of cumulous cloud. To the north, the clouds merged into a dark gray line against the horizon.

The jolt as they splashed into each new lake was always in the same direction and of much the same force: Ajão estimated that they were heading steadily southeastward. There was something else that didn't change from jump to jump: a tiny, camouflaged boat always sat in the water a hundred meters away when they popped into a new lake, and always disappeared in a great gout of water just before their own boat jumped. Apparently they had an escort.

Another jump . . . and the pressure in his ears was sudden, painful, and increasing. Ajão swallowed rapidly, found himself just barely able to compensate for the rapidly lessening air pressure. He opened his eyes, looked across the water. This lake was small, a nearly perfect circle. Broad-leafed tropical vegetation bordered a sandy beach. Mansions of pink-and-white marble were scattered through the greenery up the precipitous hillside.

For the first time in several minutes, Leg-Wot spoke. "You really think the Azhiri teleport by thinking pure thoughts, Bjault? I'm not so sure. If it is a natural mental ability, then it seems to me that the trick should cost almost no energy to perform."

"Yes. That would be the simplest assumption, anyway."

He leaned forward, trying to see as much of the landscape as possible.

"But this last jump took us up a good thousand meters. You felt your ears pop, didn't you? This barge we're on must mass better than a hundred tons. Do you have any idea how much energy it would take to lift it a kilometer? Teleportation or not, that's a job for heavy machinery, not a kilogram of quivering cerebrum."

"I don't—" he began, then stopped. To the left, the curving hillside was broken down almost to the level of the water, and Ajão could see out, beyond, and *down*. Far below, through that V-shaped cut, was the ocean. And on the horizon was a tiny strip of green. For a moment he just stared, unable to fit perspective to the view. Then he understood. This last jump had taken them to a lake set in the cone of an extinct island volcano.

It was hard to believe that less than half an hour earlier he had seen snow and felt a wind so cold it frosted his face.

"Well?" came Leg-Wot's flat voice.

Ajão tried to recover his line of thought. "I don't believe the Azhiri expend significant energy when they teleport things. Have you noticed that when other boats jump, a mass of water splashes out from their departure point?"

"Yes—" From across the boat, they heard footsteps and laughter. Several Azhiri, all dressed in light kilts, slipped over the railing and splashed into the water. Seconds later, Ajão saw the same three wading out of the lake toward a small group that had gathered, happily waving and shouting, on the gleaming beach. This was clearly journey's end. Hadn't Yoninne noticed?

"So," said Ajão, "I think their teleportation is actually an *exchange* of matter. When they jump somewhere, they simul-

©Beckman '86

taneously teleport the matter they displace back to their departure point." It made sense. *Something* had to be done with the air or water that occupied the destination. Otherwise, matter would be teleported into matter, with explosive results. By Archimedes' law, the weight of a boat is equal to the weight of the water and air it displaces; so when they teleported upward, the work required to lift their boat was balanced by the energy released in lowering the exchange mass to the departure point.

The guards were unstrapping the two prisoners now, pulling them to their feet. But Yoninne clung tenaciously to the conversation. And Ajão could see why now. The nobleman—Pelio—and his entourage were descending the wooden stairs from the upper decks. Ajão could see the somber, almost sullen, look on the boy's face, and hear the cheerful conversation of those around him. Poor Yoninne.

"I see what you mean," said Leg-Wot, her voice strangely tense. "So that's another reason why the Azhiri jump from water."

"I think he's coming down here, Yoninne," said Bjault.

Leg-Wot bit her lip, nodded stiffly. "What . . . what shall I do?"

"Just be friendly. Try not to tell him too much about our origins, at least until we're sure the Azhiri really are technologically backward. But most important, *get that maser*."

Pelio and company had reached the first deck and were walking purposefully toward the Novamerikans. Finally Yoninne said softly, painfully, "Okay . . . I'll try." For an instant he thought she might break beneath the pressure of her embarrassment and fear, but then their guards urged them to attention, and they were confronted by Pelio.

Five

One of Pelio's favorite places was his study in the North Wing of the Summerpalace. The room was an intricate melding of blackwood and quartz. It perched near the crest of the tree- and vine-shrouded ridge that ran all the way around the North Wing's private transit lake. From one window he could see the white sands and palms surrounding that lake, while from another he could look over the ridge at the ocean below, and the strip of green that was the coast of the southern continent of the Summerkingdom. The room had been designed so that a warm breeze always floated from one window or another, and no matter what the time of day, sunlight filtered down upon his writing desk in shades of green.

There were many rooms in the palace that had better views, and there were many rooms more finely constructed and more beautifully furnished. But *this* room was something none of the thousands of others were: it had been designed especially for him and his . . . peculiarities. Pelio was eternally grateful that his father permitted him quarters that, by the standards of imperial architecture, were so grotesque. (Or perhaps the king simply realized that with this room it would be easier to keep the prince out of the public eye.) Whatever the reason, the study had been a wonderful gift: it really wasn't a single room, but was partitioned into five separate chambers, connected by *doorways*—just like some peasant's hutch in the far north, where transit pools were an uncomfortable inconvenience.

Thus the "study" was actually a bedroom, a dining room (with iceboxes that could store up to a nineday of meals), a library, and a bath. Once within his study, Pelio was independent of the servants he normally needed simply to move from one room of the palace to another. Often the prince-imperial stayed ninedays at a time here, alone except for Samadhom and the servants who brought food.

Now Pelio sat at his blackwood writing desk with its glasslike surface and engargoyled drawers, and tried to find just the right words to put across the deception he was planning. The first part of the letter came easily. It was in the antique format prescribed by royal etiquette:

To: Our noble cousin Ngatheru-nge-Monighanu-nge-Shopfelam-nge-Shozheru—

Actually, Ngatheru was in the fifth tier of the peerage, but on the other hand, he did hold a direct commission from King Shozheru. Besides, it should flatter the old scoundrel to be addressed with only two names between his and the king's.

From: Pelio-nge-Shozheru, Prince of the Inner Kingdom, Emperor-to-be of All Summer, and First Minister to the King-Imperial.

That last title was an archaic touch, but perhaps it would give Ngatheru the idea that Pelio had been delegated the royal powers usual to an heir apparent of Pelio's age. Hopefully, the baron-general was far enough from the gossip of the court that he did not realize just how completely Pelio was frozen out of the ruling circles.

> On this seventh of the fifteen nineday of Autumn in the Year of Shozheru 24, we bid thee GREETINGS:

So much for what came automatically. Pelio's pen poised above the vellum. The sap oozing from the pen's cut nib had almost hardened before he set the device back in its holder. He was at a loss for words; rather, he was terribly afraid his lies would be transparent to Ngatheru. The girl's dark, elvish face rose from memory to blot out the letter before him. She had been so reserved when he talked to her on the yacht yesterday. She carried herself like one freeborn, as though she didn't even know she was a witling. She spoke respectfully, but he almost had the feeling she thought herself superior to those around her. Both she and her immensely tall companion were strange creatures, filled with contradiction and mystery. All of which added to his resolve to keep her near—even if it meant lying, even if it meant usurping the royal prerogative.

Pelio sighed and retrieved the pen. He might as well get something down. After all, he could always redraft the thing before he sent it. Begin with the usual flattery:

> Your continued command of our garrison at Atsobi is a great comfort to us, good Ngatheru. We still remember with pleasure your eviction of the Snowfolk squatters

near Pfodgaru just one year ago. Our northern marches are often perilous, and we have great need of someone with your vigilance to stand guard there.

In particular, we took note of your alert interception of two trespassers on 4/15/A/24. As you know, the king is ever desirous of having current and—as nearly as possible—firsthand knowledge of such activities. So it was that we took it upon ourselves to visit Bodgaru and assume personal custody of the captured individuals.

That was a neat touch. Without quite saying so, he had managed to imply that his father was behind his actions. The only danger was that the baron-general might have already reported the capture. But that was unlikely. Cousin Ngatheru had a reputation for independence—some might say treasonous arrogance. He did his job well, but he liked to do it all by himself. Chances were he had planned to keep his discovery secret until he had the whole affair wrapped up in a pretty package.

Pelio wondered again who had sent him the anonymous message describing what Ngatheru's men had found in the hills north of Bodgaru. Obviously, someone was trying to manipulate him, just as he was trying to manipulate Ngatheru. But who? If Ionina and Adgao had not been so patently alien, he would have suspected the whole affair was an intricate trap, set perhaps by his brother and mother. Pelio shook his head and returned to the letter:

As you know, Good Cousin, the circumstances of this incident are mysterious and ominous.
    We feel

How wonderfully ambiguous the royal "we"!

that this matter must be handled with complete secrecy and at the highest levels. Any spread of information concerning this capture would endanger All Summer.

Threatening Ngatheru with high-treason charges should help keep his mouth shut.

Pelio finished with "Abiding affection and highest regard," and signed his name. Actually, now that he looked at it, this draft didn't seem too bad. He folded and refolded the triangular vellum until it was a ball less than two inches across. Then he dipped it in a reservoir of blood-warm sap at the corner of his desk and impressed the royal seal upon the bluish resin.

Samadhom slept near his feet, a golden hulk on the sun-warmed floor. The watchbear didn't stir a hair as the prince crossed the room and pulled on the cord that emerged from a hole in the wall. Through the warm morning air came the clear sound of the bell set in the servants' room down the hill. The ringer was something Pelio had invented himself, though he felt no pride for having done so: few people ever had use for such an invention. But without that bell and cord, he would needs be surrounded by his servants every minute.

Samadhom raised his head abruptly to look at the transit pool set in the floor at the middle of the room. *Meep*, he said questioningly. A second passed and a servant splashed lithely out of the water to stand at attention at the pool's edge.

"Two things," Pelio began with the casual abruptness of one who is rarely disobeyed. "First, have this message sent to Baron-General Ngatheru at Atsobi." He handed the man the ball, its resinous covering now completely dry. "Second, I wish to question the"—*carefully!* he thought to himself. Be properly casual— "the female prisoner brought here yesterday."

"As you say, Your Highness." The man disappeared into thin air, not bothering to use the transit pool. *Show-off*.

In a matter of minutes, his letter would be packed into the softwood hull of a message torpedo, and in a single jump teleported six leagues north, all the way to Ngatheru's command bunker deep within the Atsobi Garrison. There, the shattered remains of the torpedo would be hacked apart and his message retrieved.

So much for the baron-general. If that message didn't keep him quiet, nothing would. A much greater danger to Pelio's plans lay in servants' gossip. Fortunately, he could always rotate his household servants. The ones who served him now were from the royal lodge at Pferadgaru, way south of the Great Desert. Of course they knew he was a witling, but they didn't know what little say he had at court. It should be many ninedays before they realized he was involved with a commoner witling, and even longer before they started gossiping outside their own group. Before that happened he would rotate them back to the marches of the Summerkingdom.

But Pelio saw that no matter how he worked it, he was running a terrible risk. It was always an embarrassment to the royal family when a prince dallied with a commoner. But if the commoner were a witling, embarrassment became scandal. And if the prince himself were a witling, then scandal became an eternal blot upon the dynasty. Should his deception be discovered, he would never be king.

And there was just one way his father could remove him from the line of succession. . . .

Six

There was splashing from the pool and three guards dragged Ionina from the water. Pelio grimaced. He had not even senged the imminence of the arrival. Usually he had *that* much Talent.

The four stood at attention now. "Leave me to question the prisoner," he said to the guards. One man started to protest, but Pelio interrupted, "I said, leave us. This is a matter of state. In any case, I have my watchbear."

The guards withdrew and Pelio found himself staring at the girl. She wore the same black coveralls as before, only now they were soaked. The water dripped slowly down them to pool about her boots. What should he say? The silence stretched on for a long moment, broken only by the buzzing and crooning of gliders in the trees around the study. He knew how to order his servants, how to cajole his father, even how to manipulate lesser nobles like Ngatheru—but how do you speak to a prospective friend?

Finally: "Please sit. You have been treated well?"

"Yes." Her tone was quiet and respectful, though she did not acknowledge the difference in their rank.

"I mean really?"

"Well, we would like more to live in a house with doors. You see, we can't, we can't—what is your word for it?"

"Reng?"

"Yes. We can't reng. To us, a room without doors is a cage. But then Ajão and I are prisoners, are not we?"

Pelio looked back into the clear brown eyes. Was she a prisoner? He had thought of stories to satisfy the court and Ngatheru, but had never considered just what he would tell her. "You are my guests, both you and Adgao," he said, trying to imitate her pronunciation. "For now you must stay at the palace, but eventually, I hope"—*you will want to stay*—"I hope you will be free to leave. In any case, you will not be harmed. Whatever rough treatment you have received followed simply from your secretive entry into our kingdom."

"But we never meant you harm. We're not knowing what is right and wrong with your people."

"Frankly, Ionina, I believe you." He tried once again to identify the girl's accent. He had been to most places this side of the Great Ocean, but he had never met anyone whose pronunciation was so correct—if northernish—and whose syntax was so poor. "But we're a bit curious about travelers who come from so far away that they don't know our customs. And considering the practically supernatural circumstances of your capture, we become even more curious. So I—as prince-imperial of Summer, that is—want to know as much about you as I can. . . . Isn't that natural?"

"Yes."

"Will you answer some questions then?"

Pause. "I will do my best."

"Good." Suddenly Pelio saw that he had taken the right tack. It *was* important to know more about Ionina and Adgao. Even if she had been as ugly as the man, it would have been important. He had inspected the strange devices Ngatheru's men recovered, and he had heard about the flying monster. These two were associated with powers that might make the Guild itself look puny. For a moment his conscience twinged painfully: Adgao and Ionina could be a threat to All Summer. Pelio tried to ignore the feeling. After all, he was in a position to question them. "First, Ionina, we wish to know just where you come from."

This time the girl paused even longer. She sat stiffly on the carven bench, the water dripping slowly from her black suit. Her eyes followed Samadhom as the watchbear snuffled curiously around the bench. Pelio was almost jealous for a moment. The animal rarely showed interest in other people. Samadhom must sense the peculiar similarities between the girl and himself. Finally the watchbear put his massive head on her lap and looked up through his furry face at her. *Meep?*

The girl patted the animal's head, then looked back at Pelio. "Up there." She raised her slim arm and pointed vaguely through the window at the sky.

Pelio felt an angry flush start up his neck. From one of the moons? She couldn't be. It wasn't that the moons were unattainable; the Guild could reng objects to and from them. But the moons moved at marvelously great speeds. To jump to either of them was as suicidal as teleporting to the antipodes. But he had to ask.

"From the moons?"

"No. Much further."

Further? The sun? The planets? The Guild itself could not seng so far. "Where exactly?" he asked.

Her back straightened slightly. "I . . . cannot say."

"Cannot or will not, Ionina?" He almost forgot her beauty then, so intense was the mystery she had created. He half-rose, leaned toward her across his desk. "This is something I will know, Ionina. Where are you from?"

She spoke sharply in an unknown language. She no longer seemed shy. The soft brown contours of her face were suddenly smoothed hardwood, and her eyes said, "Bring on your torture. I will say nothing more." He felt like the character in the children's tale, who captures a woods-elf and then is driven mad by her obstinacy and beauty.

As Pelio sank back into his chair another idea occurred to him. He watched her closely as he said, "I'll wager you're afraid the Summerkingdom would invade your lands if we ever figured out where they *really* are." Did she tense slightly at the suggestion? "In fact, I would wager you are of a race of witlings, hidden away in some obscure corner of the world."

"Witlings?"

Pelio almost laughed. "What you are: a person who can't teleport, who can't even keng a sandmite from ten feet."

The girl just smiled, and now her eyes told him nothing. Pelio was uncertain. For an instant there, he had been so sure. But then, he had always dreamed that there might be such a race: a people who were crippled every one, living on some island on the far side of Giri. And Ionina would make an ideal citizen in such a dream kingdom: she was a witling yet she behaved like a freeborn.

Pelio sighed. "Very well, Ionina, I won't bother you with that question"—*at least for a while*. "I'll even save my other questions. And I do have many more: we haven't even begun to talk about the flying and crawling monsters that accompanied you. But as I said, you are a guest here. I am willing to trade you information. You have already told me something about yourself; now would you like to see the rest of the palace?"

She nodded. "You are sure to show me this won't hurt the safety of your kingdom?" Somehow she managed to sound both sardonic and shy at the same time.

"Oh no." He laughed. "We are so strong that we do not need any deep secrets." He rose and motioned her to follow him to the wide marble sill of the north window. The girl walked with her usual strange grace, visible even through the bulky, dripping costume. Pelio touched the dark green garment spread out in the sunlight upon the windowsill. He had appropriated the dress from the wardrobe of his statutory harem. The fabric was so finely woven that it had a sheen whether wet or dry. And in either state it would be comfortable and light. The styling was simple, with only a single beading of rubies along the upper hem, but all in all it was the finest dress Pelio could give the girl without exciting comment among the servants. He raised the green softness from the windowsill and handed it to her. "This is for you."

"Why, thank you." She held it upside down as she inspected it. "But . . . what is it?"

The question surprised him. He could never really think of her as a savage. "It's a dress, of course." He turned it around in her hands, until it was correctly positioned before her body. "See, the upper hem goes here, and the rest just drapes down." His hands moved close to her, but didn't quite touch. "You can put it on in the alcove."

Ionina said something unintelligible. She seemed to be fighting with herself, and her large brown eyes avoided his. Then: "May I still own the clothing I wear now?"

Pelio tried not to show his anger. "Certainly."

The girl nodded and disappeared into the alcove. How could someone so graceful wish to dress like a sod?

A minute passed and Ionina stepped from the alcove: the dress revealed that she was even more beautiful than her coveralls had hinted. She stood with her long, slim legs tensed and her arms akimbo, and looked defiantly back into his gaze.

Pelio restrained the words he felt rising with him. "The dress does you well, Ionina. You look a proper guest of the prince-imperial." He pointed to the silver brooch on the curve of her thigh. "This fastener should be turned about, though. There. Are you ready to see the palace?"

She nodded uncertainly and raised her damp coveralls. "Just leave them on the windowsill," Pelio said as he pulled the servants' bell. "I promise they won't be disturbed." Before he had finished the sentence, his two bodyguards were out of the water, and standing at attention before him. Without their renging he couldn't travel the palace any more than Ionina could. "To the South Wing," Pelio addressed the men, "the Gallery."

The Gallery was as far south of the equator as Pelio's study was north, a total distance of more than sixteen hundred miles. When Pelio and the others bobbed to the surface at their destination, the floor and the surface of the pool seemed canted—which wasn't surprising since they were now almost twenty degrees of latitude away from the North Wing. Ionina pulled herself from the water, and stood for a moment on the balls of her feet, uncertain about the sudden change in the direction of down. Pelio and the others scrambled out, leaving Samadhom alone in the water, his two front paws up over the ledge of the pool. The animal kicked vigorously, and uttered furious but faint *meep meep* sounds as he tried to get out. *You overfed dummy*, thought Pelio, as he grabbed the watchbear by the scruff of his neck and slid his 150-pound body onto the floor.

The Gallery sat in the lower foothills of Thedherom mountain. The view wasn't as spectacular as many around the palace, but that was one reason Pelio chose to visit the place: with the reception for the new Snowfolk ambassador taking place up in the Highroom and the Keep, the Gallery should be uncrowded today. He was right. In fact, the only other group he could see was a collection of young nobles picnicking some five hundred feet away across the living balcony that was the Gallery.

The prince led Ionina off the stone platform and onto the grass. The green was deep and soft beneath their bare feet, and spring rain had left a sheen of water over the grass and hedgework. Behind them, the bodyguards stayed within sight but just out of earshot. Pelio pointed to the hillsides of red-flowers stretching northward up Thedherom's skirts. Those bloomed only through the spring and summer, but when the colder seasons came here, one could still find them—along with spring and summer—back in the North Wing. To the south, away from Thedherom's snow- and cloud-capped peak, green plains lay out almost to the horizon. There they merged into a faint band of dusty brown— the Great Desert, where lived the Summerkingdom's most persistent enemy. Pelio did not dwell on the thought. In his opinion, the people of the sands were low and primitive. They constituted a threat to his kingdom only to the extent that they harassed the far fiefs. Still, it was painful to recall that up until two generations before, the Great Desert had been a loyal—if nearly vacant—county of Summer.

Ionina didn't pay much attention to the band of desert. She pointed at a group of tiny figures perhaps a mile away, just where the foothills of Thedherom finally leveled off into the plain.

"Pilgrims," said Pelio. "They're walking here along the Dgeredgerai Road."

"They are witlings, then."

"No. Probably they are soldier- or servant-trainees." Most normal Azhiri spent a good many ninedays of their lives in pilgrimage, for—unless you were a Guildsman—it was simply impossible to teleport to a destination more than a few yards away, unless you had actually traveled to that destination previously. Back when his father could still hope Pelio had a usable measure of Talent, the prince had himself walked the north-south length of the palace, a full sixteen hundred miles. He had learned the palace's true immensity, but little else. Oh, afterward he could occasionally seng the pools along the line of march—which would have been impossible without the pilgrimage—but he still could not teleport to them. It was humiliating, though Pelio had plenty of servants who could teleport him wherever he wanted to go—and really, most people depended on professional rengers for long-distance jumps, anyway.

They spent an hour exploring the Gallery's fountains and garden rooms before they finally returned to the transit pool and jumped eight hundred miles northward—all the way to the triple-canopy rain forest that covered the equatorial portion of the Summerkingdom. Here he showed Ionina rooms built in the branches of the hardwood trees that rose from the steamy depths. They walked a wide avenue planed from the surface of one of those branches and listened to the buzzing and screaming of life below them in the greenish dark. Unidentified smells, both enticing and faintly repulsive, floated up past the gray-green pillars.

Pelio let his mouth babble on, but all the time another part of him was watching the girl's reaction, and admiring her dark slenderness. She listened closely to everything he said, and when she asked a question it was always intelligent—though often naive. Every so often he noticed her quietly appraising look, and wondered what judgment she was forming of him. She didn't gawk at what he showed her, as he had often seen minor nobles from the outer baronies do, the first time they saw the palace. Somewhere, he guessed, she had seen things more impressive. But where? Samadhom at his heels and the guards further behind were completely forgotten.

For midday meal, they stopped at the hunting lodge overlooking the Dhendgaru plains. The dining hall was virtually empty: with the nobility attending the ambassadorial reception in the Keep, he and Ionina had an unprecedented opportunity to roam unremarked through the palace. Pelio did not like to think of the dark side of this: the fact that his father had not required him to attend the reception was just another indication of how far Pelio was removed from the centers of power. When someday he *did* succeed to the crown, he would be the first figurehead monarch in centuries.

Ordinarily the thought would have turned him silent, but today it didn't really seem to matter. Their sauced bvepa was delicious, though the girl didn't finish her serving. She seemed more interested in the silvery sweep of the grain fields far below. Pelio found himself telling her how all those thousands of square miles were harvested and the grain teleported to the forests where it fed the animals that ultimately

© Beekman '86

provided the food they were eating. From her questions Pelio gathered that where she came from, the farmers kept their livestock in artificial containments and fed them from closed fields. It all fitted his theory: only mental cripples would have to concentrate their food production so.

Seven

The afternoon was spent renging about the palace. No room was more than one league from any other, so that even though the palace stretched eight hundred miles north and south of the equator and thirty miles east and west of the royal meridian, they could visit any place within it in two or three jumps. The hours passed and the shadows lengthened. Through the long windows of the game room, Pelio could already see the colors of sunset in the west.

He looked across the gaming table. Ionina sat hunched forward, concentrating on the silver balls Pelio had just set rolling on the table. She seemed to sense his attention and looked up. "Is there anything more you'd like to see after we finish this match, Ionina?"

The girl sat up abruptly, all thought of the game forgotten. Her lips parted but she remained silent for several seconds, thinking. On the terrace below them, several other games were making noisy progress. Finally: "Yes. When Ajão and I were . . . got by the soldiers, they took many things that were there with us. Could I see these things? They are just poor things without use, but I feel happy to see them."

You're lying, thought Pelio. He remembered those fragments the troopers recovered. They were strange, like weird jewelry. If he had been superstitious he would have called them talismans. He looked back into her mysterious eyes—*but I'd like to play along with you*. This could be an especially good chance to find out more about Ionina's background. And even if there were some kind of magic attached to those objects, it shouldn't hurt for her to *see* them. The only problem was that he had secreted them in his personal cache in the palace Keep. Pelio looked over the railing at the nobles on the terrace below. The crowd had been growing during the last hour. Judging from the shadows outside, and the formal clothes those people wore, the reception was over, its participants dispersed: it should be possible to enter the Keep without having to talk to too many people.

"I think we can do as you ask, Ionina—if you describe to me the function of these things you had with you."

The girl bowed her head a fraction of an inch, didn't look him quite in the eye. "As far as may be, I will."

They had to make several intermediate jumps to accommodate themselves to the thinning air, before they finally emerged into the gray chill of the Highroom. The room was ten thousand feet above sea level—and the most secure place in the palace, outside of the Keep itself. Down beyond the vertical slit windows a sheer cliff fell away for thousands of feet. Only a Guildsman could teleport himself to the room without first climbing here as a pilgrim. Five centuries before, when Pelio's ancestors had ruled only the Inner Kingdom, and when that kingdom had been scarcely bigger than a modern duchy, the Guild had been hired to provide the rulers with some retreat reasonably safe from attack. The Guild had senged this niche in the cliff face, and had teleported workers here to carve out the room and the yard-wide stone stairs that led three thousand feet down the cliff. Anyone climbing those stairs was helpless against attack from above, so the early kings had had no trouble excluding unwanted pilgrims. It had taken the kingdom more than a century to pay off the debt the Guild's service put upon them, but the price was worth it, for the Inner Kingdom then had the most secure redoubt on the continent. Without that redoubt, the dynasty that had culminated in Pelio and that now ruled most of one continent and part of another, would never have survived. In the end, of course, such hidden rooms became a common feature of even minor states, and the means of besieging and seizing them became widely known. That was why in modern times, the Highroom was used merely as the entrance to a much more secure volume—the palace Keep of the Summerkingdom.

The air was cold here; the room was near the equator, but that didn't offset the effect of altitude. A frigid draft eddied through the narrow wall slits. The room had been carved into four subrooms, altogether large enough to hold several hundred people and substantial provisions. Of course the place hadn't been used as a redoubt for centuries, and now it stood cavernously empty, silent but for the wind from beyond. Three soldiers, dressed in appropriately heavy clothes, stood near the windows. Pelio glanced at the men, saw that none of them wore a chief attendant's sash. He walked quickly from the pool, and peered into the other subrooms. Bvepfesh, where was the chief attendant?

Finally he returned to the soldiers. "Where is he?" said Pelio, trying to keep the pique from his voice.

The men snapped to attention. "He?—the chief transit attendant, Your Highness? He was called within." The fellow paused and Pelio could almost see the thought in his eyes: *If you were a proper heir to the crown, you wouldn't need servants to shuttle you in and out of your own Keep.* "He should be back at any moment, however, Your Highness."

Pelio turned wordlessly away, and drew the girl off to one side of the room. For a moment he just glared at the scene.

"What is the matter?" Ionina asked softly. She stood shivering, her arms folded across her high breasts.

Pelio looked across at her soft brown face, and felt the anger drain from him. "At the moment there is no one here who can reng us into the Keep."

Ionina frowned. "But you told me . . . I mean, aren't you the oldest son of the king? Of all the people, you would know the way?"

Pelio's jaw dropped. *How can she dare to taunt me*—Then he realized with an awful shock that she didn't know he was almost as crippled as she. He lowered his head, and said quietly, "I am like you, Ionina. I can't teleport; I can't even kill from a distance." It was the first time ever that this admission had not caused him pain.

Ionina looked across the room at the soldiers and the two bodyguards; the men were talking casually among themselves. They really seemed quite bored. She absently reached down to pat Samadhom's wet hulk. "What you said before. You guess right. Where I come from, the all of us are, uh, witlings."

How casually she spoke the words! He had scarcely believed the assertion when he made it—he'd simply been voicing his dreams. Now suddenly it was reality. And Ionina and Adgao seemed so civilized; they must control some sorcery, for what except magic could raise a man above the common beasts if he did not first have Talent? He opened his mouth, but his conflicting questions and speculations reduced him to momentary speechlessness. Where was Ionina's magical land? Could he escape to it?

Water splashed from the transit pool as two newcomers entered the room and bounded to attention; whoever was coming after them must be important. There was another splash, and two more figures emerged. Aleru! Even in the dim light Pelio instantly recognized his younger brother. And the other figure—heavy, ponderous, pale-skinned—that was Thredegar Bre'en. Ever since he could remember, Bre'en had been the second-ranking representative of the Snowking at the palace: ambassadors came and went, but Bre'en always remained. Shozheru and his advisers realized that Thredegar Bre'en was anything but the congenial fool he seemed. The wily Snowman was the one sure link the Summerkingdom had in its communications with the arctic lands. No matter which clique was in power at the poles, Bre'en always seemed to rank high in its councils.

Aleru was talking to the other even before they were out of the water. "And I tell you Bre'en, this is serious. We're tired of you people supporting this illegal immigration to the Great Desert. The Sandfolk attack on Marecharu Oasis cost us lives." After them, four men—all dressed in heavy Snowfolk leggings—climbed awkwardly from the pool; these were Bre'en's personal servants.

It took only those few sentences for Pelio to realize that

Aleru was speaking directly for their father, the king. But by tradition, the office of direct spokesman should go to the king's firstborn son, as soon as that son could be considered responsible. Pelio swallowed hard, and stepped deeper into the shadows, and wished he were invisible.

The motion must have caught Aleru's eye, for the other's head snapped around to look directly at them. "Who—Pelio!" The younger prince straightened his shoulders and hailed the elder: "Brother." Beside him, Bre'en bowed slightly.

Pelio returned the greeting, and tried to look self-composed. Their father had often remarked how similar in appearance and voice he and his brother were. It was true: except for Pelio's one "tiny" deficiency, they might have been the same person. But that deficiency and the accident of his being born before Aleru meant that they had always been separated by a wall of mutual envy—and hate.

Aleru was one of the few people who knew Pelio well enough to see through his deception.

His brother glanced briefly around the room, and seemed to guess that Pelio was stuck here waiting for the chief attendant. He looked back at Pelio and shrugged as if to say, *You pitiful, embarrassed fool.* Then his jaw sagged a fraction as he finally noticed Ionina's slim, dark form in the shadows. He looked at her for a long moment, and Pelio could almost imagine his futile effort to decide where in the world the girl could be from. Even the Snowman, Thredegar Bre'en, seemed interested now—though his gaze was a bit more affable and relaxed than Aleru's. Pelio tried to outstare them. After all, to explain anything at all about Ionina would imply that there was something special about her. But finally he felt forced to speak. "Do you like her?" he said, trying to smile. "A new concubine. The gift of some baron south of County Tsarang." The more obscure her origin the better. Tsarang was on the other side of the world, so far from the Summerkingdom proper that its loyalty was scarcely more than lip service. And the lands around it were wild enough to produce a creature as strange as Ionina.

"Very nice, brother. Someday I would have one."

"Certainly." Pelio nodded, and the two brothers stared at each other. With Samadhom's defensive screens hanging invisibly around them, Aleru had no way of senging that Ionina was a witling. But that didn't help matters much. Aleru knew that Pelio rarely used his statutory harem, that he despised the girls and they despised him. So Aleru might reasonably conclude there was something special about this particular girl. Would his brother guess the one terrible peculiarity that might interest Pelio?

Finally Aleru snapped to attention—an exaggerated gesture of respect—and said, "By your leave, brother." He turned and walked to the edge of the pool, then noticed that Bre'en had made no move to follow.

"Ah, yes, Your Highness," Bre'en said to Aleru. "Could we finish our discussion later? Certainly the ambassador should hear what you say firsthand. And I don't often get the chance to speak with the prince-imperial. If he is someday to rule All Summer, then we of the Poles must know him."

Aleru pinched in one side of his mouth. "Do whatever you please, Bre'en." He dived into the pool and disappeared.

For a moment after Aleru's party left, no one spoke. Behind the Snowman, his servants stood at blank-faced attention. Quite likely, they were witlings; no person with Talent could be as completely intimidated as a witling. It was rumored that the Snowking valued fear and oppression so much that he was systematically breeding a race of witlings to rule over. In the long run such schemes were laughable. In the short run they were ghastly grotesque, even to Pelio.

Bre'en smiled, and leaned forward to gesture Ionina out of the shadows. "I am captivated by Your Highness's acquisition. She is beautiful—almost supernaturally exotic. Tell me, little one," he addressed the girl, who was anything but little, "to reach the Summerkingdom from County Tsarang you must have crossed the Snowkingdom. Did our land please you?" For all the man's ugliness, he had an engaging smile.

The girl seemed puzzled by his question, finally said faintly, "I no . . . I mean, I don't know."

Bre'en's laugh was cheerful, yet not mocking. "You don't know? In just four words my entire kingdom is consigned to obscurity! I am crushed." He turned to Pelio, and abruptly changed the subject. "Your Highness, it was not by our request that we deal with your father through Prince Aleru rather than yourself."

Pelio nodded woodenly. Another time, he might have speculated on the Snowman's motives. As it was, the words scarcely registered.

Bre'en bowed and walked toward the transit pool. His men followed with stiff, almost awkward precision. As soon as they were gone, Pelio started for the pool himself. Ionina caught up and said, "We go to show me those things now?"

The prince shook his head abruptly. "No. Later, it will have to be later." To his surprise, she seemed more upset by his refusal than by anything else that had happened. His hand came up and he almost patted her shoulder. "Really," he said in a more kindly tone, "we'll do it another time. Soon, I promise." But the promise could be an empty one. If Aleru suspected Ionina was a witling, he might check Pelio's story; if he looked hard enough, the story would collapse. And that would be the end of them.

Eight

By the time Yoninne arrived at the prison-cell-*cum*-guest house, twilight had darkened into night. One of the moons had risen over the rim of the ancient volcanic cone, and its silver-gray light sparkled off wavelets in the central lake, limned the sloping sides of the boats floating there, and turned the beach she walked along into a pale, curving strip. From somewhere across the lake, still in the shadow of the cone's wall, there were sounds of laughter and splashing, and a pleasant smell that could only have been barbecue.

One of her guards — guides? — drew her off the sand onto a path that angled up the hillside into the palmlike trees. The moonlight scattered into triangular silver fragments as it sifted down, and the smell of green things hung all about. In the humid air, her dress was only beginning to dry, but the material was so soft and light that she scarcely noticed the dampness — while the flight suit she carried in one hand was still sodden, even though it had been lying on the windowsill all day long.

This was quite a change from her treatment that morning, when she had been hustled off a straw pallet in a doorless cell and unceremoniously hauled from one pool of water to the next. Now her guards were almost solicitous; after Pelio said good night they had even agreed to walk her to her quarters rather than teleport there.

Ajão had certainly been right about the boy Pelio. As the number-one son of the biggest wheel on the continent, he was spoiled rotten, but it hadn't taken long to see that behind his bluster was a kind of soft-hearted naiveté. That had puzzled her through most of the day until, there in that strange cold room, he confessed that he couldn't teleport any more than she could. You'd think he was admitting to some terrible disease; poor guy, in a way perhaps he was.

That admission was just further evidence that the Azhiri needed no super-technology. Sure, they had simple crafts—ironworking and such—but all the fantastic things they did were applications of the "Talent" most of them were born with. She hadn't really been convinced of this till she saw what passed for toilet facilities among the upper classes; the fixtures were carved from marble and quartz, yet the waste-disposal system was no better than a common outhouse.

All in all it had seemed safe to tell Pelio that no members of her race could teleport. And her admission had made the kid look so . . . happy.

Through the leaves and tree trunks she saw a flicker of yellow. The path wound on another fifteen meters, then opened onto a clearing set in the hillside. By the moonlight she saw a large cabin done in the usual stone-and-timber style—but this building had a *doorway* hacked through one wall. The flickering light from within painted a yellowish trapezoid on the mossy ground.

As she stepped into the fresh-cut doorway, Ajão Bjault looked up from the wall torch he had been examining. "Yoninne!" After a day filled with gray-green faces, his chocolate skin and frizzy white hair looked incongruous. The old man's gaze flickered from Yoninne to the two Azhiri who still stood in the darkness beyond the room. "I didn't hear you coming up. Are you all right?"

Yoninne smiled. Ajão's hearing was so bad he would probably miss the crack of doom. She stepped into the room. Behind her, she heard the two guards retreat. "I'm fine. Just fine."

The other looked at her a bit strangely. "How do you like this place?" he said. "They brought me here just before sunset. Quite an improvement." Yoninne looked around. Like most isolated buildings she had seen that day, it had only one room, with a transit pool in the center. Pelio had been as good as his word: their new apartment was nowhere near as opulent as his quarters, but it looked comfortable enough. Yoninne curled up on one of the pillowed chairs and suddenly felt very tired in a kind of satiated way. Supper had been *good*. The lead and mercury in the local "edibles" would be lethal in the long run, but they certainly didn't affect the taste of food.

Ajão still had a puzzled expression on his face. "I've been trying to make these torches burn brighter," he said. "They're not just simple pieces of wood. They have a wick structure. . . ." He stepped back from the torch's wall bracket and peered out the doorway into the darkness. Then he turned back to Yoninne, "I don't know why I'm so cautious; they don't understand a word I'm saying." Now that she looked at him more closely, she realized he was tired and jittery. And still he had the air of being unable to believe what he was seeing. "Did you have any luck, Yoninne?"

"Luck?"

He frowned. "The maser, Yoninne. The maser."

"Oh, no. But don't worry, we'll get it some other . . ." Her voice stuttered into silence, and her peaceful mood vanished as abruptly as if she had been slapped in the face. She understood now the puzzled look in the other's eyes, and realized just what he was seeing: Yoninne Leg-Wot, the stubby, flat-chested pilot. She looked down at herself, saw the thing she had called a dress—a short green kilt, barely large enough to hold her wide hips. She had been running around like a fat-assed fool all day. Leg-Wot bounced onto her short legs, felt a hot flush of humiliation rising to her face. And this senile bastard just stood there pitying her.

"God damn you, Bjault," she choked out as she stumbled across the room to the lavatory alcove. She yanked the curtain shut and ripped off the skimpy kilt. Her flight suit was still damp, but she pulled it on with a few quick motions, and zipped the diagonal fastener. She stood silently for several seconds watching herself in the wall mirror. Wearing the flight suit, she was her usual coolly efficient self.

She slid the curtain aside, and walked back across the room, the water in the suit's boots making faint *squishsquishsquish* sounds. The old man still hovered nervously by the far wall. "You know, Yoninne," he said in that diffident, hesitant way of his, "you're not the only person who's had a bad time today. Until this evening I was cooped up in that cell, wondering what they had done to you . . . and what they were going to do to me. I—"

Leg-Wot raised a slablike hand, "Okay, Ajão, I apologize for blowing up. Let's forget it." She settled her bulk onto the pillows, and felt the cold material of the flight suit press comfortingly against her back. "Now, do you want to hear what I've been up to today?"

The other nodded, then sat down on a facing pillow-chair as she began. "First of all, I'm convinced that your ideas about Azhiri teleportation are exactly correct. I was shuttled all over the palace today. Most of the time I could keep the sun in sight, so I was able to make rough estimates of how far and in what direction we had moved, and those estimates agreed pretty well with the 'lurches' I felt—just like you predicted." Yoninne was only an adequate computer tech, but as a "seat-of-the-pants" hot pilot she was outstanding, the best aircraft pilot in the Novamerikan colony. She had an uncanny feel for accelerations in rotating frames of reference, and this was just the ability she had used to keep track of her position today. Sometimes Yoninne wished she had lived during the time of the Last Interregnal War on Homeworld, when aerial combat made its first and only appearance in that planet's history. She could have shown those old "aces" a thing or two.

"Anyway, this Pelio kid showed me around the overgrown park he calls a palace." Leg-Wot went on to describe the places she had seen: the hedgework that girdled the side of a mountain, the mammoth treehouse. Bjault's questions brought out a hoard of detail, and they talked for several hours—till she thought the archaeologist probably had a clearer vision of what she had seen than she herself did.

The torches were burning low by the time he returned to the question he had asked at the beginning of the evening. "But you weren't able to persuade this Pelio to show you our gear?"

"Uh, no . . . and that's really a strange thing. I told you the boy is lonely, that he can't teleport himself like the others. I think I've got him wrapped around my little finger. We were actually on our way to some high-security area where they've stashed our stuff. Then these two other characters showed up; they rank lower than Pelio—one of them was his brother. But somehow it really upset him to see them. It was almost as if he had been caught doing something he shouldn't. He made up some kind of lie about who I was, but I didn't understand all the words."

Finally Bjault had no more questions. The night beyond the doorway was slowly cooling. In the silence, the faint stridulation of the lagoon's tiny mammals sounded loud. "You've done well, Yoninne," he said. "My confinement has scarcely slowed our progress, I'd wager. If you can just stay in Pelio's good graces long enough to get another crack at that maser, we'll get ourselves rescued yet." He paused, and an impish look softened the lines of strain and age in his face. "I'm just glad you don't speak Azhiri any better than you do."

"Huh? Why the hell is that?"

"Because you haven't had a chance to pick up any swear words. Your vocabulary—mine, for that matter—has all the purity of a child's. It has to, since children are about the only people we've had a chance to listen to."

Leg-Wot bit back an angry retort. She'd rather not let him see how mad such remarks made her. "Don't worry, Bjault. I'm learning."

With that the committee of two adjourned for the night. They tried to rig a curtain across the doorway, but finally had to settle on stuffing one of the largest chairs into the opening. It didn't really block the way, but it would slow anybody—or anything—trying to enter. The transit pool was harder to block, since they couldn't see how to drain it. Finally they gave up, Bjault doused the now-guttering torches, and they retired to their separate couches. Leg-Wot pulled the coverlet over her head and quietly shed the protection of her clammy flight suit.

She lay awake long after the old man's breathing became loud and regular. With the torches out, the land beyond the doorway was flooded with light. The first moon still hung out there above the cone's curving lip, but now the second, larger moon had risen, to shine several degrees above the first. They were both a common grayish brown, like the basaltic moons of a thousand other planets, but now they were so close together she could see the subtle difference in their hues. They were at last quarter but their light was so bright it made a complex net of double shadows across the broad-leafed trees that stretched downward from the cabin. The skittering and rustling continued as loudly as before. It was an altogether different music from the night reptiles of Homeworld or even the insects she had heard on Novamerika, yet it had a certain attraction.

What would she do tomorrow? She thought of the green scrap of cloth she had discarded. Unless she had broken the clasp on it, it was still wearable. But she'd be damned if she'd make a fool of herself again! That spoiled kid would just have to get used to her wearing a flight suit. Leg-Wot felt her teeth gritting together, and tried to relax. She knew how much was at stake here, how important it was to play up to Pelio. Without him, they would be without protection, and—more important—they would have no way of recovering their equipment. If word didn't get back to Novamerika, it might be more than a century before the new colony would risk its

resources by landing here again, more than a century before they would discover this world's great secret.

She glared out onto the moonlit landscape. There was really no help for it. After all, it hadn't killed her to wear the thing. *Pelio* obviously didn't think she looked ridiculous, and he was the person she had to manipulate. If one more day's humiliation was the price of getting that maser, then she would pay it.

Nine

This time there were no hitches. Again they went to the place Pelio called the Highroom, but now they found the special servant who could jump them into the Keep itself: they emerged from the transit pool into a vast, pale-lit emptiness. The wan light came from scattered greenish patches that seemed to float in the dark. It took Yoninne several seconds to realize that those patches were the same funguslike material that had hung gangrenously from the walls of their dungeon in Bodgaru. But this place didn't stink, and the floor was dry and unslimed beneath her feet. The room was an ellipsoidal cavern so long that the glow patches on the far wall were little more than green stars in the dark. Their transit pool was set on a fifty-meter-wide ledge that shelved out from where the cavern's wall began curving over into the ceiling. Abruptly Yoninne realized that nearly half the greenish lights were actually reflections in an oval lake that filled much of the cavern's floor. The water was so still that she might never have noticed it if she hadn't seen the faintly reflecting hull of a boat moored against the near shore.

They started down the steps that led from the shelf. As usual, Pelio's servants trailed a fair distance behind. "This is my family's Keep," said the prince with evident pride, "probably the best angeng" (?) "in the world." She had a hard time following the rest of his description; there were too many words that she did not recognize. But she was able to piece together the overall story. Originally the Keep had been a natural cave, with only one small entrance, and that near the Highroom. The Guild had senged (felt? seen? sensed?) the cave's location and sold the information to the Summerkingdom. Pelio's ancestors had entered the cave and enlarged it to its present size. The single entrance had then been blocked. From then on, security was relatively easy to maintain: the Azhiri could not teleport to any point that they could not seng. And if you weren't a Guildsman, the only way to seng a location was to travel—by some means other than teleportation—to within a few meters of it. After that, apparently, the spot could be senged from any distance.

Once in every generation, the passage from the Highroom to the Keep was unblocked. New members of the royal family climbed the narrow stairs that led up the cliff to the Highroom, and then walked down the passage from the Highroom to the Keep. A very few trusted servants—those destined to become Highroom attendants—accompanied them on the second leg of their pilgrimage, but only those of royal blood ever made the entire trip.

Most of the palace servants had made the pilgrimage up the stone stairs to the Highroom, so they could teleport themselves and—if need be—their masters that far. The Highroom attendants could then teleport the visitors inside the Keep. It sounded like a pretty good system: except for the royal family (and the Guild, of course), no one could get all the way into the Keep without another's help.

"And the lake? Why is that there?" asked Leg-Wot as Pelio's talk petered out. The boy still seemed friendly—after all, he had agreed to take her here this morning—but he was a good deal quieter, more nervous than before. Sometimes she thought he didn't even want their conversations overheard by the bodyguards. She didn't know what to make of it, and now that they were so near her goal, it was beginning to get on her nerves.

Pelio looked at her as she spoke, and his face creased with a shy smile. By human standards that face was strange—all round, with scarcely a chin or a point of a nose—and she wasn't sure quite how to read it. Certainly no other person had ever looked at her the way he did. "The lake is for transport. We're within one league" (one jump?) "of five different royal roads, so the members of my family can come quickly into the Keep even from outside the palace. That's the whole point, you know: the royal family must have some retreat safe from all attack—a Guild attack excepted, of course."

There it was, that "Guild" again. Sometime, she was going to have to learn more about that organization. But right now, she was much more interested in getting at their equipment; even with the maser they might have problems calling for help. It wasn't a matter of power: Novamerika was at conjunction, not more than fifty million kilometers away. The maser could easily punch through to any medium-sized antenna at that distance—if the antenna pointed in her direction. But what if she and Ajão and Draere's people had all been given up for dead? Then, the only time the Novamerikan colonists would aim their receivers at Giri would be to monitor the robot telemetry station Draere had left on that godforsaken island on the other side of the planet. She might have quite a problem synchronizing her transmissions with that station.

Once on the Keep's main floor, Pelio guided them around the edge of the lake. The four-footed ball of fur that Pelio called Samadhom kept right at their heels.

Her eyes were adjusted to the dark now, and the place seemed like an open harbor lit by hundreds of tiny green moons. The air was not absolutely still; a faint draft riffled gently by her dress. The walls of the cavern swelled inward to the central lake, forming little hillocks along the floor. Pelio pointed to the holes in the walls. "Most of the rooms here share the air of the entire Keep. It's too much trouble to reng fresh air into each room separately; the fewer servants allowed into the Keep, the better. And in general, no foreigners get in except when we have diplomatic receptions here. My family stores too much of value in the Keep to let just anyone enter." Yoninne almost smiled at the unconscious pride of his tone. He was so self-contradictory. "I've had everything that was found where you were captured put in my own storage room." They turned right and moved away from the central lake. In the dim green light she saw the rock rising on either side of them: they were walking up a miniature valley cut across the long axis of the Keep. The "valley" narrowed till it was more like a hallway without a ceiling. Finally they came upon a small transit pool.

Pelio said, "We could have jumped directly here, but I wanted to show you the Keep." He turned to the guards as they caught up. "Jump us into my storeroom," he said quietly, pointing at the nearest wall. "It's about twenty yards in that direction."

The shorter of the guards shut his eyes in concentration. "I seng it, Your Highness," he said softly, matching Pelio's tone. Somehow even small sounds seemed loud in the emptiness.

They slipped into the pool and emerged seconds later from a similar one in the interior room. The green-lit room was crowded with wooden cabinets and bronze bowls—the bowls filled to overflowing with what must have been gems and precious metals, though in the dull light their sparkle and flash were muted. Yoninne looked across the tangled heaps of treasure. The place was more like an unkempt attic than anything else. What was the use of all this stuff if they kept it hidden away?

Pelio started across the room, then came to an abrupt halt. The others piled up behind him, looked down, and saw the bodies. There was not a mark on them and their kiltlike uniforms seemed in perfect order, yet they lay on the floor like puppets with cut strings. One of the bodyguards pushed past Pelio, knelt beside the bodies, and felt for a throat pulse.

"They're not even warm, Your Highness. Shall we sound alarm?"

"Yes—no!" The boy clenched and unclenched his hands. "Stand outside the room now. I must think—I mean, I must inspect the room for loss."

"But, Sir—"

"Go!" he said. The two guards snapped to attention, but left only after they had convinced themselves no one was hiding in the room.

After they were gone, Pelio stood for a long moment as if dazed. Yoninne looked at him, then at the bodies. "Were they murdered?" she asked.

The prince nodded abstractedly. "Kenged, I should think," he said, then noticed her blank look. "Someone jumbled their insides." He said something else she couldn't understand, but it sounded like cursing. "I just don't see how something like this could happen *here*, in the Keep." He was talking to himself now.

Samadhom sniffed mournfully around the bodies, as if trying to wake them. Yoninne looked abruptly away. The Azhiri race didn't need knives or pistols; their Talent was enough. Those two men—servants by the look of them—had simply been . . . turned off. Draere's death had been bad enough, but at least it hadn't been murder.

You sentimental fool. Get off your tail and find that maser. The thought brought her back to her normal, efficient self. It was just her luck that when she finally got near her goal, some palace intrigue would get in the way. She moved closer to Pelio, and said, "The equipment? Where is that stored?"

Pelio glanced up, pointed carelessly at a cabinet across the room. It was a big one, more than four meters on a side. Its massive, deeply carved door was ajar and through the opening she could see a jumble of parachute fabric. The sight affected Pelio, too. "That door should be closed!" He strode swiftly across the room, Leg-Wot close on his heels. The prince pulled the door open wide and they waded through the knee-deep fiberene chute material. The ablation skiff and the burned-out hulk of the motor sledge sat within the cabinet, along with a rack of empty metal trays. A cold and unpleasant certainty was forming in Leg-Wot's mind; most of their equipment had burned up with the sledge, but the maser and the machine pistols, at least, should be here. She scrambled around the side of the skiff to look in the hatch. Even in the dim light she could see it was empty. There were the sealed instruments and the web restraints, but that was all. The maser was gone. Gone.

She described the missing items to Pelio. "I had those all put here," he said, pointing at the metal trays. From the stricken look on his face, she knew this was not some elaborate game he was playing with her. "So they killed to get just those things. . . . But how could anyone steal from the royal Keep?" His eyes widened. "Unless the thief were a Guildsman . . . or a member of the royal family."

Leg-Wot turned angrily away from him. Now she and Bjault really were marooned—and under a death sentence to boot.

Ten

That morning Ajão Bjault pretended to be asleep as Leg-Wot rose and dressed in the skimpy green kilt she had worn the night before. The pilot was exceptionally quiet and Bjault guessed she would be just as happy if he didn't wake. After she was gone Ajão got up and washed in the room's primitive lavatory. A few minutes later, two servants emerged from the transit pool with breakfast. The food didn't taste bad, though the thought of the insidious poisons it contained made him want to gag. Bjault finished the meal and watched morosely as the servants slid back into the water and disappeared. It was all very well that Leg-Wot was having so much success with Pelio, but he was going out of his mind with boredom and suspense.

He stepped into the morning sunshine, and walked down the path toward the beach. The sky was filled with a rippling of clouds, and it wasn't quite as tropically warm as the day before. This place was beautiful, there was no question about that. And it was beginning to look as if he had all the time in the world to explore it; except for a small group lounging on the beach a quarter of the way around the lake, there was no one to stop him. Perhaps he and Yoninne weren't really prisoners anymore. Only his inability to teleport kept him prisoner here: he couldn't enter a single building—except that one they had punched a doorway in.

Bjault walked along the edge of the woods, and listened to the animals scurrying back and forth among the wide-leafed tropical trees. They seemed relatively tame; he had seen several hop across the narrow path. Ahead, a mouselike creature spread a silken web between two trees. It was an amazing fact: Ajão had seen no animal life that didn't look mammalian. Oh, most of the ecological niches were filled: there were "birds" of sorts, and from the finned monsters he had seen in Azhiri murals, he knew there were sea creatures. But the birds had fur and suckled their young, and the sea monsters were clearly air-breathers. There was even an insect analog here on Giri, though up close the creatures looked more like miniature shrews.

Bjault could think of only one explanation for all this. Back fifty or one hundred million years ago, Giri had had reptile and insectoid forms, and the first mammals were coming on the scene. But one of those mammals was a mutant like none ever seen on any of the thousands of worlds man had visited: this animal could teleport—"reng" was the Azhiri term—matter. Certainly the creature hadn't been able to teleport itself; probably the best it could do was reng tiny masses just a few centimeters. But consider: if the matter teleported was within the brain or the heart of an enemy, then that enemy would most likely be killed. So the lucky renging mutant was the undisputed master of its environment. Considering how rare the mutation must be, it was not surprising that no other species ever learned to use the Talent or defend against it. All other macroscopic fauna had been wiped out, and now every creature was descended from that single fluke. Bjault shuddered.

Of course the Azhiri race itself had come along millions of years later, just as *Homo sapiens* had only developed in the latter stages of mammalian evolution. But where their animal precursors could teleport only a small fraction of their body mass, a trained Azhiri could reng whole tons. At least most Azhiri could—Pelio was an exception, a cripple. Apparently, he couldn't even defend himself against the Talent.

Bjault noticed a small transit pool half-hidden in the trees up the hillside. He left the beach to climb toward it. There really wasn't much reason to, but he had nothing else to do. He would just have to be patient another day or two. Leg-Wot was so close to recovering their equipment. He entered the clearing and walked to the marble rim of the pool. Leaves and other forest debris floated on the surface. Apparently this pool was little used. Bjault wondered how the Azhiri managed to avoid accidents. Sooner or later, some poor fellow would get into a pool just as someone else arrived, and be chopped in half, his lower body teleported wherever the newcomer had departed. Perhaps the Azhiri clairvoyance— "seng," or whatever they called it—was even more effective than Leg-Wot reported.

It suddenly occurred to him that there was another reason why accidents didn't happen. It takes energy to cut a solid or liquid, to break the molecular bonds along the surface of the cut. If—as it seemed—the Azhiri didn't expend energy to do their tricks, then there was only one way they could cut an object by use of the Talent: if the materials along the cleavage were chemically identical at both the departure and arrival points, then there was little *net* energy expense during a teleportive exchange. Thus you could reng two equal volumes of water. (Or, if you wanted to kill somebody, you could reng two equal volumes of your victim's medulla oblongata; jumble his brain, in effect. Witlings led a precarious existence indeed on Giri.)

Bjault gazed idly across the clearing, and happened to be looking right at the man as he popped into existence, then dropped three or four centimeters onto the deep grass. The archaeologist rose abruptly to his feet, but not before two more men materialized.

"Don't move, witling," the first of them said. "The prince requires your presence." All three wore the standard kilts of the household guard, but there was something tense and furtive about them. Ajão had been dealing with bureaucratic and military types for well over a century, for so long that he almost had a feeling for their lies. These three behaved like soldiers in enemy territory. He took a step backward, toward the path that led to the beach. One of the three disappeared, popped back into existence a little way down the trail. At the same instant an incredibly sharp gust of wind struck Ajão's ankles, knocking his feet out from under him. Two of the men closed in, grabbing his arms. "We can kill you before you even start to scream. Don't hinder us, and we may let you live." Ajão gritted his teeth in pain and fear as they dragged him across the grass toward the transit pool. This was kidnapping, not the lawful activity of jailers! And the difference was not academic—he might never see Yoninne or the maser.

As his abductors reached the pool, the fellow bringing up the rear screamed, and there was an abrupt snapping sound, like nearby thunder; Ajão looked up to see the man's body smash into the bole of a tree at the far side of the clearing. Just at the entrance to the clearing was a fourth man, a dark-skinned Azhiri in a plain green kilt. He stood unmoving, but Ajão's captors went pale with fear. "Guildsman," one of them shouted, and when he looked down at Bjault there was murder in his eyes.

There was a second snap of thunder, and his would-be assassin was literally blown away. The ground slammed up against Ajão and he felt nothing more.

Beyond the railing, the city stretched as far as he could see. Individually, the buildings were beautiful, their stone and timber construction blended subtly together. Even the largest of them, three and four stories tall, were part of an immense garden. Vines and tree limbs had been guided through the latticed balconies and rooftop porches, to set off with tones of green and brown the blue paint of the outer woodwork.

It had to be a city, but no building stood closer than one hundred meters from another. Only the pathless gardens and their trees and flowers and tiny ponds lay between them. It reminded Ajão of the planned cities they were just beginning to build on Homeworld when the Novamerika Expedition was launched forty years before. Those cities had been made possible by the advanced Homeworld technology with its computer-directed helicopter transportation—whereas the Azhiri achieved the same effect without mechanical tricks. Ajão felt a little envious. Their city might be thirty kilometers from east to west, yet the Azhiri could jump from one end of it to the other with scarcely more than a two-meter-per-second jolt.

Ajão was lying on a soft couch set on one of the roof porches. Except for the soaked condition of his flight suit, and the soreness in his legs, he was quite comfortable. This was hardly a prison cell. The furniture and art work excelled what Pelio had provided them. A wide, low table sat alongside the couch. Its surface bore two circular paintings, each more than a meter across. They looked almost like maps: the blue representing ocean, the green and brown and white the land. Notations in the Azhiri syllabaric script marked various points. There were even little sea monsters painted on the blue. . . . Why, these *were* maps, polar orthographic projections! One disk represented the northern hemisphere, and the other the southern. What a strange projection to use; the equatorial continents were distorted almost to unrecognizability.

From behind him came footsteps. Bjault whirled to see— his rescuer. The fellow leaned over the couch, offered Ajão something dark and very cold. Iced drinks yet; all the comforts of a tech society. Ajão numbly accepted the glass. "Where am I?" he asked, as the other settled himself into a nearby chair. The stranger looked a bit older than Pelio, and was probably of a different Azhiri race: his skin was a very dark gray and he stood nearly 160 centimeters tall, rather big and lean compared to the other natives. His green kilt had a stylized pair of silver moons stitched across the side.

"Near the center of the business district of Dhendgaru, right here," he said, pointing to a gray splotch on one of the maps. He moved his finger about a centimeter. "And here is the Summerpalace, less than two leagues away. You haven't been moved far . . . and you are free to return." He looked up abruptly at Ajão. "But I must speak with you first. My name is Thengets del Prou, second Guildsman resident in Dhendgaru."

Ajão's ears pricked up at the word "Guild." "Thengets del Prou," he pronounced the words carefully. "I'm Ajão Bjault."

Prou smiled. "Even if you didn't look like an outlander, I'd have known you weren't from the Summerkingdom. Summerfolk have considerable trouble with the hanging consonants in my name."

"Then you aren't native to this kingdom yourself?"

"Oh, no. I was born in the Great Desert, the second son of a chiefling among the Sandfolk."

Bjault remembered what Leg-Wot had said about that race. "Aren't your people, uh, great enemies of the Summerkingdom?"

Prou's grin broadened. "They certainly are. And I'd probably be a combat leader crawling through the sand to raid some Summerkingdom oasis, if I hadn't been destined for the Guild. But I don't remember my family. I was less than a year old when the Guild took me. It was a lucky thing, too: occasionally the Guild will miss a child, which can be horrible for the village he's born into. There are cases of super-Talented kids just taking over isolated villages, killing anyone who opposes their whims. Children like that should be raised by equally Talented adults—Guildsmen—who can plant consciences in them."

Prou slouched down in his chair and hooked one bare foot over the edge of the map table. He had none of the severe formality Ajão had seen in other Azhiri. Prou seemed to be one of those people who does his particular job very well, and has a lot of fun with that job and the rest of the universe. In fact, his casual nonchalance reminded Bjault of some of his wackier grad students, years ago on Homeworld.

Ajão tried to suppress the natural liking he felt for the man. Was there any objective reason to trust him? The archaeologist sipped at the sour alcoholic drink and tried to disguise his indecision. What could explain Prou's appearing just in time to rescue him from the kidnappers?

"You must have been watching me for some time," Ajão said finally.

The Guildsman hesitated a second, then nodded. "I was at Bodgaru when you were captured. I tried to get to you before the Summerking's troops, but it was just too risky. The local prefect was watching me pretty closely."

Ajão raised his eyebrows. "I was told the Guild was beyond laws and governments."

Prou laughed. "It may seem that way to some people. Certainly we have physical power. We can seng everything on Giri and even on the moons, so we can teleport objects anywhere in the world without first making a pilgrimage to both the departure and destination points as a normal person must do. We dug the transit lakes simply by renging down rock from the moons. And if it ever comes to a fight, a single Guildsman can destroy whole cities the same way."

There was no boasting in Prou's tone—and Ajão realized he was telling the literal truth. If a hundred-ton moon rock were exchanged for an equivalent volume of—say—air at Giri's surface, the net potential energy released would be equivalent to a small fission bomb. Perhaps that explained the glassy plain Draere had photographed in the southern hemisphere.

"But," continued Thengets del Prou, "do you know how many Guildsmen there are—in the whole world?"

Ajão shook his head.

"Less than six hundred—and a quarter of those are children. Six hundred out of four hundred million normal Azhiri. Yes, we do have power, but at the same time we abide by the Covenant. If ever the commoners and the kings' armies united against us, they could destroy the Guild, though the price would be millions of lives."

A three-way balance, thought Ajão; *the Guildsmen with their terrible powers, the national aristocracies with their well-trained armies, and the commoners with their numbers*. Any two could successfully gang up on the third. So every kingdom—no matter how feudal its structure—must treat its subjects with some justice. And between kingdoms, open war was to be avoided, since it would weaken the aristocracies relative to the Guild and the commoners.

"And that's really why you and your lady are so important, Adgao. You are witlings, yet the powers you were playing with up in Bodgaru were as great as any Guildsman's—I saw the flying monster Ngatheru's troops shot down. One way or the other, your existence will change all the world. I want that change to be for the better . . . or perhaps it would be more objective to say that I want to have some control over how things change. In any case, I couldn't let the Summerking-dom's intelligence arm have you to themselves: I sent Prince Pelio an anonymous letter describing your capture. The prince is fairly powerful, and certainly the greatest eccentric in the court. I was counting on him to keep you out of Ngatheru's hands. Then I could contact you, try to persuade you to put yourselves under Guild protection. Pelio couldn't complain about the arrangement to his father without reveal-ing his own misdeeds, and I was sure you would go along once you saw how much safer you'd be with us."

Ajão disagreed but remained silent. No matter how un-certain a patron, Pelio had the maser, and that was their only salvation.

"But I never realized," the dark-skinned Azhiri continued,

"that someone else was playing the same game. You probably guessed those were not Summerpalace guards who attacked you. They were expert soldiers, though: all three could teleport themselves without a transit pool. Whoever was behind them wants both you *and* your equipment. I'd give a lot to know just who it is: Prince Aleru? Someone in the intelligence arm?"

But Ajão scarcely heard Prou's speculation. "Our equipment? What about it?"

"Pelio stored it in his private room in the palace Keep. I was in the Keep yesterday, attending a very dull reception King Shozheru held for the Snowfolk ambassador. I snooped around—something Guildsmen are peculiarly equipped to do—and found the prince's private room. But I was too late. I found two dead servants there—they weren't too late; they must have surprised whoever was going through Pelio's room. As far as I could tell, the thieves took everything of yours they could carry."

The revelation was a ragged knife stuck through Ajão's middle. "What?"

Prou nodded. "I looked everywhere." He described what he had seen, and Bjault realized he was talking about the ablation skiff and the wreck of their powered sledge; someone had taken all their loose gear—the maser included.

The Guildsman saw the look on Ajão's face. "I'm sorry too, Adgao. But my offer still holds. If you and your friend wish, I will take you away from Pelio and the court. Otherwise, the royal family will eventually discover that Pelio is consorting with witlings, and when they do, you two, and even the prince, will be in mortal danger."

Ajão shook his head weakly. "You don't understand." *You don't understand; we'll be dead in a matter of months if we can't get off your wretched world.* They had lost their only means of calling for rescue, the only radio on the planet with sufficient power to—His eye caught on the planetary map that covered the table beside him.

But there was another radio! There, at the edge of the monster-speckled blue ocean was the island where Draere's people had set up the telemetry station. The place was a quarter of the way around the world and surrounded by thousands of kilometers of water, but if they could somehow get there . . .

If we only had an aircraft. If the colonial administration on Novamerika had let them have all the equipment they needed, they wouldn't be in this mess now: the ablation skiff was no flyer, it was hardly more than a heat shield and a parachute. It had brought them safely down from orbit, but now it was good for nothing.

He looked up at the Guildsman. "You said the Guild can teleport things anywhere on Giri?"

"Yes."

"Perhaps we can make some sort of deal, then. As you suggest, we do understand, uh, magic that is unknown to the Azhiri. We would explain some of that magic if you would teleport Yoninne and myself here." He reached across the map table to tap the island where Draere's telemetry station stood.

Prou frowned, and Ajão wondered if he would value what little Ajão could reveal to him. There was simply no way the Azhiri could be taught anything of modern technology in the time that remained to Yoninne and himself. The machine pistols might be worth something to Prou, but they were gone now. About the only equipment they could offer him was their suit radios, whose range wasn't much over fifty kilometers.

But that wasn't Prou's objection. "I could certainly teleport you there, Adgao—but you'd die on arrival. Look." He sketched the line connecting Dhendgaru with the island. "The distance is more than one hundred leagues. One league is the farthest a normal road boat hops in a single reng—even with the heaviest hulls, no boat can safely jump more than two leagues at a time. You would be smashed into many small pieces if I renged you there."

Ajão studied the map, and grimaced. Of course. The telemetry station was a quarter of the way around the planet. If they jumped there from here, they'd come out with a relative velocity of nearly a kilometer per second—directed downward. But still . . .

"What's to keep you from taking one of those road boats out into the ocean? I realize now it would be a long trip, probably several hundred jumps, but we'd eventually get there in one piece."

Prou shook his head again. "These abvom"—he tapped one of the ornate little sea monsters painted onto the map's oceans—"aren't here just for decoration, Adgao. They'd keng us before we got three leagues out to sea."

It made sense. If the ability to keng depended—as it apparently did—on brain size, then seagoing mammals could well be the most deadly creatures on the planet, even if they could not teleport themselves. No wonder the Azhiri "roads" never cut across more than a few kilometers of open sea. Ajão half-rose from his couch. "But if the place is so inaccessible, how do you even know it's there!"

Prou's gray eyebrows went up. "We in the Guild can seng it. Just as we can seng the moons—even though we can't take ourselves there, either."

Bjault sank back onto the couch. In effect the telemetry

station was as far away as Novamerika itself. For a moment he wished he had Leg-Wot's flair for obscenity. This was an occasion for it.

He looked down at the map. At first glance, the polar orthographic projection seemed a terribly awkward way to map an entire hemisphere. The lands within thirty degrees of the pole were relatively undistorted, but toward the equator, the continents were so foreshortened that—on this map—all the Summerkingdom occupied a strip less than eight centimeters wide along the edge of the disks. Then Ajão realized that the projection would look quite natural to Azhiri eyes; it was peculiarly suited to their unique Talent. For them it was more important to know the *velocity difference* between two points than to know the actual distance between them. And the polar orthographic projection was a perfect representation of the velocity field of the planet's surface. Straight lines on the map were not great circles, but they were paths of least speed change between the points they connected, and hence—from the Azhiri point of view—the shortest paths. That finally explained the strange curves the roads followed; if only he'd had this insight back before Draere tried to land.

The more he looked at the map, the more he realized how apt it was. You could see at a glance how many jumps were required to reach a destination safely, even tell the magnitude and direction of the jolt experienced on each jump. And it showed just how impossible it was to get to the telemetry station. Even if they traveled overland to the point closest to the station, there would still be an 8,500-kilometer stretch of ocean between them and their goal. If they took that in a single jump they would emerge at the station moving horizontally at several hundred meters per second. There simply was no way, unless . . .

"By God, that's it!" Bjault said in Homespeech. He would never have seen it without this map, yet a born Azhiri would never have seen it without Ajão's technical background. He looked up at the puzzled Guildsman, and said with a triumphant grin, "Between your Talent, and my 'magic,' I think we *can* get to that island!"

Eleven

They called it the Festival of the Southern Summer—and ignored the fact that this marked the shortest day of all winter in the northern hemisphere. It was the greatest of the imperial holidays, equaled only by the Festival of the Northern Summer a half year away. The present affair wasn't quite up to previous years—the duchies Rengeleru and Dgeredgerai were too busy holding their trade routes through the Great Desert against Sandfolk incursions to send their usual shows to the court. Nevertheless, most of the Summer peerage had come to the fest, filling all fifteen tiers of the Equatorial Amphitheater. The amphitheater was a natural ridge line stretching north and south some five hundred yards. It had taken the king's laborers more than three years to carve the brownish-pink rhyolite of the hillside into fifteen shelves, each for a particular degree of nobility. Then millions of tons of topsoil, turf, and trees had been laid over the steps until an occasional pink streak of polished stone was all that showed through the green.

It was just two days since the mysterious invasion of the Summerplace Keep had been discovered. Though nothing had been revealed publicly, the rumors had spread—and the guards posted at every transit pool and ornamental pond of the amphitheater simply strengthened the rumors. Pelio wondered if things would ever return to normal. It had been a miracle that he was able to get Ionina out of the Keep unnoticed; he had never seen his father's advisers so upset. Even though they found nothing missing from the king's private rooms—and Pelio didn't admit to his own losses—they were still faced with the irrefutable fact that someone had taken advantage of the diplomatic reception to rifle the Keep, and murder two air-rengers. The would-be thieves had had great Talent and incredible audacity. From that night on, patrols roamed the Keep, the first time any king-imperial had ever thought that necessary.

But only Pelio realized the true enormity of what had happened. Only Pelio knew that the thieves had actually stolen anything; someone had penetrated the Keep, someone who could reng objects out of it without the aid of the Highroom attendants. A Guildsman—or what was more likely, considering how carefully the Guild abided by the Covenant of Powers—a member of the royal family. The prince kept this knowledge to himself. He knew his situation was precarious; questions were being asked that might incidentally expose his relationship with a witling commoner. For a few days he must avoid the girl, both in public and private.

Pelio drifted from conversation to conversation, ever standing on the outskirts, and never knowing quite what to do. It had been different before he met Ionina. Then, he had been content to sulk. But now that he knew how much fun the give and take of conversation could be, he couldn't do that either. Perhaps it was just as well: he looked across the terrace at Aleru and Queen Virizhiana. Whoever burgled his storeroom was playing a deadly yet mysterious game. Until he knew more about that game, it was wise to remain quiet and inconspicuous.

He moved away from the crowd, and walked to a tree-enclosed bower near the edge of the terrace. Here the smell of flowers and green leaves was stronger, and the sounds of the fest fainter. Just a few inches from his feet, the grass ended abruptly and the ground fell steeply away, exposing the polished pink bedrock. From where he stood, Pelio could see every one of the fifteen tiers, all the way down to the baronial level. But there was so much greenery that he could see only a fraction of the crowds.

Somewhere under the trees on the ninth terrace, the fest's musicians struck up "Invitation to a Joust." On all the terraces the crowds moved forward to watch the action on the jousting plain to the west. Pelio's little bower was invaded by a trio of young nobles, full of chatter and wagers. By the blue in their kilts, Pelio knew they were from some country court and rightly belonged down on the sixth terrace. But the fest's formality was not strict, and with the proper friends a nobleman could go practically anywhere in the amphitheater. For the first time in years Pelio found himself unrecognized, and before he knew it, he was betting his largest ring that one Tseram Cherapfu would carry the day on the field below. In fact, he knew nothing of Tseram Cherapfu; it was a name he had heard discussed earlier by some other jousting experts.

The four settled down in the soft grass to watch the event. Seconds later the two contenders appeared—one at the north end of the plain, and one at the south. At this distance they were tiny specks, distinguished only by their colorful jousting costumes. Pelio gathered from the others that the red-suited fellow, the one on the north, was Cherapfu.

A crack of thunder broke across the plain, and dust billowed up from the turf near the jouster dressed in blue; Tseram Cherapfu had taken the first shot. One of the young nobles snorted that such a premature attack was a foolish waste of effort, and another responded that you could never be sure, that Cherapfu was sometimes uncannily accurate. The two figures walked slowly toward each other, till they were barely four hundred yards apart. Now the thunder began again, but this time it continued in a ragged staccato of sharp snaps, the sound of super-velocity air slamming into existence above the plain.

The contest was a friendly one, but these men fought as trained and talented soldiers would in a real battle. For in actual warfare, it was usually impossible to scramble your enemy's insides by a direct application of the Talent: unless he were dazed or a witling his natural defenses would protect him against a keng attack. So it was necessary to assault the enemy indirectly, by teleporting air and rocks from many leagues away, air and rocks that would emerge traveling hundreds of feet per second in the direction of your target.

The battle in the plain below could not be quite so realistic: the contestants were not allowed to reng solid projectiles and their air blasts emerged high above the ground. Still, it was spectacular: the sledgehammer winds drove grass and dust up into dirty clouds over the field as the two troopers flickered back and forth, trying to avoid each other's blasts.

Pelio found himself yelling just as loudly as the others.

They were good, those soldiers—even he could tell that. Both had made the Grand Pilgrimage through the arctic to be able to reng in the thunder like that. And only a few highly trained people could jump without a transit pool, yet these men were doing so every few seconds.

It couldn't go on for long; the soldier in red staggered beneath a multiple series of blasts that flattened the grass around him. He swayed dazedly, defenselessly, as the thunder converged upon him. The four boys sucked in their breath at once, as a final blast knocked Cherapfu backward. He did a complete flip before falling to earth.

A cheer swept the length of the amphitheater, and the three boys jumped to their feet, arguing excitedly about the match. Pelio found himself talking, too, parroting back arguments he had heard earlier in the afternoon. And strangely enough, it was fun, even though he didn't understand half of what he said. As Pelio slid the ring his wager had cost him off his finger, a second wave of cheering sounded behind them. They turned to look through the trees. The winner of the match had just emerged from the main transit pool, to be greeted by Alcru and Virizhiana, and receive the wreath of victory across his blue jacket. The crowd closed in about them and—

Ionina! She stood about twenty yards from the pool, and right next to her towered the gangling, brown-faced Adgao. How could they possibly be here? Who had brought them? His amazement was drowned in the chill fear that this time he could not possibly carry off his deception. Pelio numbly turned back to the others and handed his ring to the nearest of them, then walked out of the bower, with Samadhom close on his heels.

Behind him he heard one of the boys exclaim, "Jiru, look! The prince-imperial's seal is carved into this thing."

I've got to get them out of here, got to get them out of here. It was all Pelio could think as he walked across the grassy terrace toward the girl and her grotesque companion. There were first-rate troopers all around, people who could seng for a certainty that these two strangers were witlings. He couldn't be seen talking to Ionina.

Then he realized it didn't matter anymore: the terrace was strangely silent. Even the talk around the transit pool had died. He and Ionina and Adgao had become the center of attention. He saw now that the two aliens were actually in the custody of guards. There was no more hope. Pelio straightened his back and slowly walked the distance that separated him from the girl. It was so quiet he could hear his feet parting the grass, hear voices from the terraces below. How ironic that things should come to an end now, on such a sunny, blue-skied day.

Finally he stood facing Ionina. She seemed to catch the fear he felt, though she couldn't know the cause. Behind the guards stood three of Pelio's household servants. They must be responsible for bringing Ionina and Adgao to the fest. Were they bungling fools—or had someone put them up to this? The question rippled the top of his mind, but deep down he knew it didn't matter.

There were sounds behind him, and when he turned he was not surprised at the tableau confronting him. There was his father, the king. Shozheru's mouth opened and closed, like a sea-bat out of water, as he vacillated between mortification and rage. On either side of him were ranged his advisers—those grim-faced, loyal men who all these years had urged their king to remove Pelio so that Aleru could succeed to the throne. To one side stood Aleru himself, his

gray-green face blanched almost white by—what? Rage? Triumph? In the crowd behind them, only two or three faces caught Pelio's eye: his mother, her gaze fixed on some point above his head; Thredegar Bre'en, his face as bland as ever; and Thengets del Prou. The dark-skinned Guildsman had always been strange, one of the few persons who talked to Pelio as if he were no different from everyone else— perhaps because, from Prou's superior vantage point, Pelio wasn't that much less Talented than the normals. But now even that dubious ally seemed far away and indifferent. It was the whole world set against himself and the two other witlings.

At last old Shozheru found his voice, though it quavered with pain and anger. "*Why*, Pelio? You could have been king of All Summer . . . at least in name. I had managed that." His voice croaked away into silence, then began again. "All, *all* you had to do was to keep some shred of dignity about you, to pretend that my dynasty could continue through you. Instead, you surround yourself with de—degenerates." He pointed spastically at the tall strangers standing behind Pelio. "If I let you succeed me, your 'court' would be the laughingstock of All Summer. What vassal could even pretend loyalty to you? The empire would fall in a year— though it has stood five centuries." And now the pain seemed much stronger than the rage. "What choice have I, Pelio? By law you must succeed me, or you must die. After this"—again he gestured at Ionina and Adgao—"you can never succeed me."

A soft yet defiant voice spoke from behind Pelio. "There is other choice." Ionina's interruption stopped Shozheru cold. No nobleman had ever addressed him so abruptly, much less a commoner, much less a witling. Pelio turned to look at the girl. Ionina was not cringing. She looked levelly at Shozheru, and her strange beauty held him motionless. But when she spoke again, her words broke the spell—in fact, provoked quickly suppressed laughter through the crowd:

"Pelio will travel across the Great Ocean soon, and you will have rid of him."

The king-imperial's body straightened as he gathered his powers. "Do not mock me!" His voice was shrill and womanish but there was death in his face, and at that moment Ionina should have fallen dead, the interior of her brain or heart jumbled into a nonfunctioning mess. Instead, Samadhom gave a pained yelp and rushed clumsily to her side.

The girl continued, her voice tense and argumentative. Didn't she know how close she'd come to death? "I do not mock you. I speak truth."

Shozheru came down from his rage, his body bending back into its usual infirm posture. For the first time he seemed aware of the onlookers. He glared weakly at the three witlings and said, "We will discuss this in private. Now."

The crowd parted silenty before them as they walked to the transit pool.

———

Shozheru's study was in the western foothills of the palace mountains. Beyond the open windows, brightly lit greenery stretched half a mile to where the land dropped away to the depths of the equatorial rain forest. Inside, the room was plain, its only ornamentation a collection of small paintings—portraits of Shozheru's forty-seven predecessors. Even the table at the center of the room was devoid of the carven gargoyles so popular nowadays. Except for the addition of four portraits, the room had remained unchanged for nearly a century, since the Teratseru period—when simplicity had been thought elegant.

The study was very crowded at first, before the king ordered his advisers and all the guards to leave. In another time, Pelio would have been greatly amused at those advisers' consternation; they came close to angry argument with their king. But finally they left. Only five people were left then: Aleru and the king on one side of the room, and the three witlings on the other.

Shozheru set his palms on the deeply varnished surface of his desk and stared at his son for a long moment. The king seemed more rational, more resolved than before. "She says I have a third choice, Pelio." He didn't look at Ionina as he spoke. "She says you are going to 'travel across the ocean,' and leave the way to succession open to Aleru."

Pelio looked down the table at Ionina and Adgao. The girl looked back at him with that dark, mysterious gaze of hers, and Pelio knew she hadn't been mocking anyone: her witling kingdom must lie across the sea and she must know a way to get there.

"Yes, Sir, that is true," he said.

"How?" The single word was loaded with infinite sarcasm; there were lands beyond the oceans, but no one—not even Guildsmen—could safely go there. Pelio opened his mouth, but no words came to mind.

"I will tell you how." The girl's voice was so soft, yet as decisive as before. Shozheru's eyes swung unwillingly toward her, but this time he listened.

And Ionina told them. In some detail. A chill crept up from the pit of his stomach as she spoke. The scheme was insane; how could even magic make it work? Shozheru and Aleru listened expressionlessly but from their brief questions

Pelio could tell they also thought the plan was a shortcut to a particularly unpleasant death.

When Ionina finished, Shozheru turned back to Pelio. "It would be suicide, son," he said quietly. "Is this what you three really plan to do?"

What is the alternative? thought Pelio. He knew that Shozheru was convinced now that Pelio couldn't rule Summer even as a figurehead king. That meant that Pelio must be removed; Pelio must die. Exile was not sufficient—so unbreakable custom dictated—for princes can always come out of exile with insurrectionist armies. . . .

Yet no man had *ever* returned from across the sea, no man had ever survived a jump even one-tenth so far; the king could probably persuade his advisers to let Pelio undertake that journey, rather than have him executed.

"Yes, Father," replied Pelio; but he doubted that—even with the faith he had in Ionina and Adgao—he could ever have accepted their scheme, if the alternative were not an imperial death warrant.

Shozheru looked down at the table. Behind him, Aleru stared through his father into the distance. It was obvious they understood the situation. This way, at least, the king would not have to be his own son's murderer. "Very well," Shozheru said at last. "I grant you three all the freedom the girl has asked for, all the materials, and all the labor." He looked up at them, and Pelio realized that his father was making an expensive gesture in granting Pelio's "wish." The Summer court was already the butt of ridicule for the way it pampered the witling prince. "You have nine days."

The king walked across the room and slipped into the transit pool without a word of farewell.

"I will send for your servants," said Aleru as he too started for the transit pool. He hesitated by the water and turned to face the witlings. His head was silhouetted against the bright greenery beyond the windows, so Pelio couldn't see his features. Was there a tinge of mockery in the words he spoke? "However this turns out, the dynasty will be saved, brother. But I hope that . . . somehow . . . you will succeed."

Twelve

They began their journey the morning of the seventh day after the Summer Festival. The sky was inauspiciously overcast and a warm drizzle slid down the sides of Pelio's yacht as it floated in the North Wing's transit lake. Yoninne Leg-Wot looked across the puckering water at the gray beaches and rain-slicked vegetation. There was no one to see them off. All that morning, as they finished their departure preparations, she hadn't seen a single servant or nobleman except those assigned to Pelio's project, and even they seemed sullen. This didn't bother her, but Pelio took it all kind of hard. Since their confrontation with the king, many people weren't even pretending respect for the prince. Pelio's disgrace went so deep that he was almost like an "unperson" in some totalitarian state. And if they couldn't accomplish Ajāo's plan in the nine days Shozheru had given them, Yoninne had the feeling they would all be dead unpersons, to boot.

Nine days. When Bjault and the Guildsman had first described the plan, that had seemed an awfully long time. She had soon found out how wrong she was. With all necessary equipment and technical support things would have been easy, since basically Ajão's scheme was very simple. But in many ways the Azhiri technology was stuck in the iron age; even the simplest gadgets had to be made from scratch. The ballast for instance: on that item alone Yoninne had wasted three days testing various approaches.

She had worked eighteen and then twenty hours a day; it was no use. The days passed just as quickly. And more and more, Bjault had been a drag on her progress. The old man tried to keep up with everything she did, to make her explain all the steps and procedures. She was rid of him only when he slept and during those hours he spent working an interminable Runge-Kutta analysis of the plan. At one point he had the entire desk and much of the floor covered with papers bearing his neat, pen-scratched mathematics. In a way, she had to admire Bjault for that: most of Leg-Wot's contemporaries would be at a complete loss if they couldn't solve their differential equations on a computer—they would never think of doing something like that by hand. But Bjault had been an adult before the reinvention of digital computers, and when he orginally learned his math, numerical analysis had all been done by hand. Still, it was an irritating waste of time; Leg-Wot had *told* the old man over and over again that his plan would work. She had known that the moment he described the scheme. It wasn't that she was a mathematical genius—she just had a feel for certain things.

But they had had several things going for them: the Guild's secret assistance, an endless supply of hand labor, and—through Pelio—the authority of King Shozheru. Eventually they had licked all the preliminary problems; they were ready to begin the first, and safest, part of Ajão's plan.

The boat's warning whistle sounded. Leg-Wot slid back into her chair and pulled her harness tight. All along the deck, the crew took their places, while beside her Ajão and Pelio tied themselves in, too. The boy was nervous and tired; he had been up most of the night trying to get a couple of extra pilot-navigators. Pelio gave Yoninne a quick, nervous smile, and looked across the deck at the chief navigator. The navigator was an especially husky Azhiri dressed in baggy coveralls. The fellow never looked directly at Ajão or Yoninne, though he showed stiff courtesy to the prince. No doubt he thought Pelio was running from disgrace. The guy reminded Leg-Wot of her father: a hardcore officer willing to cooperate with his superiors' most idiotic whims.

The navigator had been a hard man to get. Only selected combat types ever made the pilgrimage across the arctic. It had taken Shozheru's authority to pry him away from Summer's army. But without him and the two other navigators, they would have to take on local pilots for at least part of their journey.

Now the man's heavy face tensed for an instant—and the first jump was accomplished. A dozen different impressions assaulted Leg-Wot's senses at once. There was a moment of free fall as the boat rose up and eastward. Then she was pressed firmly back into her seat, and the boat's timbers groaned as the yacht smashed into the destination lake. Suddenly the day was bright and cheerful, for there were only scattered clouds in this new sky.

But that was only a single jump, the first of more than a hundred. Minutes later they teleported again, and jump followed jump, till their surroundings became a surreal blur in Leg-Wot's memory. The skies stayed mostly sunny, and the warehouses at water's edge looked pretty much the same from lake to lake, but the landscape beyond them flickered from grassy plain to city, to mountains. The sun edged jerkily southward as they traveled further into the northern reaches of the Summerkingdom. Traveling by "road boat" was like a pleasant combination of flying and sailing. It was strange to remember how frightening and mysterious their first ride on one had been. Now, even that crazy boat whistle seemed both sensible and commonplace: it blew when their navigator renged air from their next destination into its chamber—the air's relative speed somehow determined the pitch of the whistle, so it was easy to estimate how much of a lurch to expect.

Two hours passed, and they stopped at a place Pelio called Pfodgaru. It was lunch time. They were pulled into a wharf and pots of steaming soup were brought aboard. Leg-Wot watched Bjault as the food was passed around. The archaeologist had been unnaturally quiet all morning; there had been none of the usual penetrating questions, none of the theories thrown off the top of his head. Now he fiddled with his soup, looked half-nauseated. He noticed Yoninne's gaze. "Cramps," he said in Homespeech, "all morning." They stared silently at each other for a long moment, and Yoninne knew they were thinking the same thought: *Metallic poisons— lead, mercury, antimony—they're in everything we eat, building toward sudden death within us. Are these the first symptoms? And if so, how much longer do we have?* Ajão looked abruptly away, then said to Pelio, "We are still within the Summerkingdom?"

The prince stared with some puzzlement at the two Novamerikans, then nodded, "We're right at the northern edge, almost thirty degrees from the equator, further north even than where you were captured, though the climate here is milder than Bodgaru's." Yoninne looked across the stone warehouses, the weather-beaten wood residences. Pfodgaru was a pale, chilly imitation of cities further south. Yet things would get colder soon: along the railing, crewmen were enclosing the deck with slatted quartz windows.

"I know," continued Pelio, "this isn't the nicest place in our kingdom, especially during the winter. But it is the southern end of the only polar road which treaty allows us to use. For the next hundred leagues—all the way to County Tsarang—we'll be within the Snowkingdom."

Their next jump transformed the mountains surrounding Pfodgaru into a tiny gray serration on the southwestern horizon. The terrain didn't seem too different from the northern reaches of Summer: there was a bit more snow, a bit less vegetation here. The towns they passed were built exclusively of stone. This was unsurprising, since there were no trees— much less forests—in the flat, gray land. Yet their stonework was different from what she had seen in the South. The designs were angular and faceted, their gargoyles more abstract than grotesque. And while the Summerfolk inevitably laid sections of different-colored stone next to one another, the Snowmen preferred the opposite effect: even when different sorts of stone were available, they segregated them so that each building was a solid shade of gray or brown.

There was a feeling of poverty about the towns that Leg-Wot had not noticed in her brief visits to the cities of the Summerkingdom. Nature made life hard for these people. Most of the buildings around the transit lakes were small in comparison to what she had seen in the South. She was certain that if Bjault had not been sick he would have been pestering Pelio with questions: How did the Snowfolk support themselves? Where did they get food? How did they heat their stone houses?

They jumped from town to town, each jump spanning perhaps a hundred kilometers. They were heading northeast now, so that every teleportation sent the yacht lurching up and eastward from the water of the next transit lake. The sun ran quickly toward the horizon. And it was *cold*. The wind keening through the window slats carried a subzero draft onto the passengers. The wood-burning deck stoves didn't help much. Poor Samadhom huddled miserably by one for a while; then Pelio unstrapped him, and moved the animal into the boat's hold.

In the lengthening, north-pointing shadows, the villages seemed grotesquely squalid. The snow piled up high around the water like some mineral deposit; many warehouses were built of dirty gray ice rather than stone. Still further north, thick ice shelves stuck out into the water. Snowmen work crews hacked industriously at the ice, trying to keep the road open. The water in the lakes was a peculiar green now; even when it splashed up on the window slats and froze, it had a greenish cast. Pelio told Leg-Wot that the Snowpeople had potions they added to the water to keep it liquid even at these temperatures. Antifreeze, huh? It was hard to believe that only a few hours before they had been traveling through semitropical forests.

Except for a thirty-degree wide band straddling the equator, Giri was a frigid world, its ice caps reaching down in places to the forty-fifth latitude. The colonists from Homeworld had been wise to settle on Novamerika, fifty million kilometers closer to the sun. The Novamerikan tropics were insufferable, but swimmable beaches extended to the poles. In the three years since the colony's establishment, she had come to love walking alone on those long, empty beaches. *But will we ever get back?*

She slumped in her chair and for a while sat as silent and withdrawn as Bjault. When she looked up again, the sun had set in the south. The twilight faded to night inside of four jumps—yet it was scarcely past midafternoon! The shifting landscapes were now lit by the stars and the fainter of the two moons. The buildings seemed more graceful, more delicately formed than they had in the failing sunlight. Yellow lamps glowed cheerily in their windows. The air was like crystal, yet the wind coming through the window slats blew steadily, strongly.

Pelio became more talkative, as if he sensed the downturn in Yoninne's spirits. He had been this way two or three times before, both on state visits to the Snowkingdom and on tours of vassal states beyond the pole. He described the functions of the various buildings clustered about each transit lake, and proudly identified the freighter traffic bound to and from the far fiefs of Summer; the sun-over-fields seal of the Summerkingdom shone on hull after hull, clearly visible even by moonlight. As they progressed into the northern night, traffic became heavier. Soon the splashing water had frozen over the windows and obscured their view. Every third or fourth jump, their pilot-navigator sent crewmen out to chip away the ice. The stoves were restoked and the tiny red sparkles leaking through their sides lit the deck.

Pelio was so animated, so cheerful that Yoninne almost smiled. No doubt he thought they would most likely die at the end of their journey, yet he was doing his best to cheer *her* up. She wondered again if he would have gone along with this scheme, if the alternative had not been execution. Nine days ago—it seemed so much longer now—when Bjault and Thengets del Prou had first put Ajão's plan to her, she had insisted that they go directly to Pelio with it.

Prou had been skeptical. "Pelio would be taking a terrible risk in cooperating with you. The Keep is rotten with guards now; if he tried to use his authority to take what remains of your equipment, the chances are Shozheru would discover he's been consorting with witlings. That would mean almost certain death for the prince—I just don't think he's willing to take that chance. We've got to create a situation where Pelio—and his father—will be *forced* to cooperate."

Yoninne had looked angrily across the tiny room at the Guildsman. Someone had murdered to get their maser; someone had come within centimeters of snatching Bjault. They were at the center of a deadly intrigue that neither she nor Ajão understood. And now this fast-talking Guildsman wanted them to betray the only dependable friend they had here. In the guttering torchlight, she couldn't read Bjault's face: did he really buy Prou's argument? How could they be sure that Thengets del Prou and his Guild were not the people behind all their problems?

The arachaeologist seemed to be reading her mind. "I think we can trust him, Yoninne," he said in Homespeech. "If he wished us ill, we'd be dead or kidnapped by now. And the help he's giving us will only serve to put us beyond his power."

"Then your pet Guildsman is doing this out of the goodness of his heart? Or did you promise him the keys to the magic kingdom?" Leg-Wot replied in the same language, her voice heavy with sarcasm. "If he's not the guy who stole our weapons and the maser, then there's nothing we could do or tell him that would be of any value."

Ajão answered quietly. "That's not so. I told Prou about Novamerika. He's almost as eager as we are to establish contact; he seems to be equal parts political realism and pathological curiosity. Do you know that for all his power, he's not allowed to travel more than a few jumps from Dhendgaru? If we get rescued, he wants passage to Novamerika."

Leg-Wot grimaced. Bjault made Prou sound like some bright college student "thirsting for knowledge."

But Ajão's plan was their only hope for survival now that the maser was gone. And that plan depended upon Guild cooperation. They had no choice but to trust Prou. She tapped her stubby fingers irritably against her chair's armrest, then turned to the Guildsman and spoke in Azhiri: "Just how do you plan to force Pelio and the king to go along with our scheme?" The word "our" came easily to her lips. From the moment Ajão had described his plan she had been sure she could make it work.

Prou leaned forward, seemed to listen for a moment to the night sounds outside the bungalow. "That's simple, though a bit risky. You'll publicly reveal yourself to be witlings, witlings intimately associated with Pelio. Shozheru will have to accept your plan, as a means of removing Pelio from the line of succession. His only alternative would be to have Pelio executed, and the king is really too good-hearted to do that. In giving Pelio this last chance, Shozheru will have to provide you with the equipment you need."

And so Leg-Wot had grudgingly accepted the Azhiri's suggestions. On the day of the festival, Prou had arranged to have Yoninne and Ajão appear right into the middle of the royal court (even though it was not apparent that he was responsible for their arrival). The guards at the transit pool had immediately recognized them as witling intruders and the confrontation they had counted on took place—with just the results Prou had predicted.

The thought brought Yoninne back to the present—to the chill night beyond the ice-splattered windows, to Pelio's young face lit by the reddish gleamings of the deck stoves. It just wasn't right: She was sure he would have accepted the plan, risks and all, if they had laid it out honestly before him. Instead they had betrayed Pelio, and put all their faith in a man who—despite Ajão's logic—might still turn out to be the rat in this affair.

Thirteen

Grechper was the largest city she'd seen since leaving the Summerkingdom. It stretched around three sides of the transit lake: first the warehouses, many three and four stories tall, and beyond them the residential and business sections, angular buildings of stone and ice separated by narrow, crooked streets. A far cry from the open cities of the South. East of the transit lake lay a jagged, tumbled wilderness, glinting here and there in the moonlight. Yoninne had little experience with arctic environments, but she recognized this: the frozen surface of an ocean, crisscrossed by faults and pressure ridges. And that was the way they would go tomorrow.

Their men marched protectively about them as they walked down the pier from the yacht. Above, the stars and moon gleamed in the crystal dark. The wind had died, but Yoninne could feel her warmth being radiated through her parka and face mask into that clear arctic night. Each breath froze into a million tiny diamonds, while beads of ice condensed around the eyeholes of her mask. Except for Ajāo, their group looked like so many moon-lit teddy bears. And the featureless lump on the litter ahead of her was Samadhom, hunkered down under a pile of blankets.

Their party proceeded up the narrow street that led from the pier. The snow and crushed ice beneath Yoninne's feet felt like sand and gravel. What a place: how could anyone bear to live here? Yet it was clear that many people did. The wharves and streets were crowded, both with locals and travelers. The Snowfolk didn't even bother with face masks.

———

The Summerkingdom's consulate in Grechper was a lone stone building that looked like a rebuilt warehouse. Inside, the halls were lined with hardwood paneling and murals depicting Summer landscapes. Firewood was imported all the way from Pfodgaru, Pelio said, to stoke the many furnaces that had been installed in the building. After the cold outside, the warmth and the sound of crackling wood were almost as welcome as a sunny day in the South. Now off his quilted litter, Samadhom padded down the hallways, sniffing enthusiastically into every room.

The place seemed queerly familiar to Yoninne; despite the climate, Grechper and the consulate reminded her of home. Here, people *walked* from building to building, and the rooms were connected by hallways and doorways rather than by transit pools. She supposed that they must use transit pools for some jobs, but in most cases—if one end of a trip were out-of-doors—it just didn't make sense to teleport.

The consulate's chief officer led the witlings up a steep stair to the second floor, where the rest of the consular staff stood nervously at attention. No one had been warned of the prince-imperial's visit to Grechper. Pelio put the staff "at ease," and said mildly, "We'll be laying over just one night—twelve hours or so. I'd like my men given hot meals and billeted according to their various ranks. My own party"—he waved his hand to include Yoninne and Ajão—"will also eat now."

The consul bobbed his head. "At once, Your Highness." The fellow was a bit past middle age, and he and his subordinates had a kind of beaten look. Their clothing was not actually frayed, but it did look old and worn. Perhaps she was wrong to think of this place as a consulate—these people looked more like overworked shipping clerks than diplomats.

And the meal they were served fit the same picture: the consul kept apologizing for not having anything fresh from the South, and his staff—doubling as waiters—hovered curiously about the dining table. For the first time the food tasted metallic, tasted as poisonous as it actually was. The only thing good about the meal was the wine, and in the end that almost made up for everything else: a pleasant warmth spread outward from her middle, and everything seemed more congenial.

All through the meal, Bjault played unhappily with his food. By the time they cleared away the dishes, he had eaten barely a quarter of his share. A sheen of sweat lay across his forehead and his hands shook faintly as he pushed his plate away. For the first time she had a gut feeling for how terribly old he was—longevity treatments or no.

Pelio followed her gaze and spoke to the guards who had stood inconspicuously in the background all through the meal. "Help Adgao to his room." Two of them raised Ajão to his feet and supported him as they sidled down the hall, with Yoninne, Pelio, and the consul close behind. They passed through a curtained doorway—even here in the arctic doors didn't seem to be very popular—and laid the archaeologist on a deep pile of pillows. All the while, Ajão protested that he wasn't *that* sick. For once his talk didn't annoy her; Yoninne knelt to loosen his collar. "I know, I know," she said. "You may still be functioning now, but we've got another two days of this to go through."

Pelio looked anxiously down at Bjault. "Yes, things are going to get a good deal more strenuous before they get easier. Do . . . do you think you'll be able to make it?" He was deliberately obscure; the consul and the guards were listening. There were good reasons for keeping their ultimate plan secret. Whoever grabbed the maser and tried to grab Bjault was still at large.

Ajão nodded painfully. "I'll go through with it even if I have to crawl. You're right . . . today was bad. But I'll get better. I just need a little rest . . . I think."

"All right. Try to sleep. If you need anything there'll be a couple of guards just outside this room." They stepped back through the curtain, and as they returned to the dining room, Pelio continued in a softer voice, "How sick is he?"

Yoninne considered. Bjault was more than 150 Homeworld years old—not counting the years he spent in deepfreeze during the trip to Novamerika. That made him one of the oldest humans in known history, so there wasn't any way of estimating how durable he was. For now, she might as well try to feel optimistic. "Don't worry. He'll recover."

Pelio brightened. "Good." He waved the others away and they entered the dining room, sat down at a corner table. Samadhom curled up under the table, his head resting on his master's booted foot. "You know, I'm almost beginning to think that we'll make it, that this whole crazy thing is going to work out. Let me show you what I suggested to the chief navigator." And he described his scheme for rotating the men from sleep, to guarding the consulate, to guarding the equipment aboard the yacht. The witlings would be safe from sabotage even if their mysterious enemy had planted several agents in the crew. It was a good plan; Pelio had taken care of just those things she and Bjault could not. The boy seemed a lot brighter, a lot more flexible away from the court of Summer. *Perhaps in the end*, she thought, *he will benefit from our scheming as much as we will.*

Their talk slowly petered out, without either of them really being aware of the fact, till they were just sitting there, looking at each other with silly smiles on their faces. *It's that damn wine*, she thought to herself, and wished she'd had some a long time before. She realized now she had liked Pelio almost from the beginning, and she realized why: he looked at her as though it were a pleasure to do so. He made her feel light and tall—as she hadn't felt since she was six years old, when her figure still fell somewhere in the range people termed "cute." It was strange: here she was, stuck in a backward corner of a backward world, with only even chances of getting home alive—and suddenly she felt less alone than ever before.

Pelio's thick hand reached across the table and closed gently over hers. "Perhaps my father's learning about you and Adgao was the best thing that could have happened to me. Oh, at the time I was scared out of my wits, and when you described your plan—then I was even *more* scared, in a way. But now I see how carefully you and Adgao have thought everything out, and I'm so grateful I was included in all this. If it works we'll find your witling kingdom, where I . . . where we can have normal lives. And if it doesn't—well, at least it will have been a spectacular try."

Later, Yoninne blamed the wine for what she said next, but at the time it was the most natural thing she could think of. "I'm glad. When we decided to have Thengets del Prou bring us to the festival, I was afraid we were just ruining your life to save our own necks."

"Thengets del Prou renged you to the festival—not some incompetent chamberlain?" Pelio spoke softly but his tone was flat.

The change in his voice barely registered in Yoninne's mind. "Prou was responsible. We—Ajão and Prou really—weren't sure you would help us unless you had no other choice. I'm so happy now that it's turning out best for you, too—"

Pelio's hand was snatched from hers as the prince crashed to his feet, half-stumbling over the drowsing Samadhom. The watch-bear gave a pained yelp and pushed himself further under the table. For a moment, Pelio just stood staring at her, his face as pale as a Snowman's. "You mean you three set me up for all this?"

Yoninne felt her skin go chill; her dreamy mood was turning into a nightmare. "But—but you just said this is better than going on with your old life!"

Pelio leaned across the table, his smooth, round face coming within centimeters of hers. He said something she didn't understand, but it must have been a curse. "Yes, I said that—and perhaps it's true. But I didn't know you had intrigued, manipulated me into this—like some child or dumb animal." His words came fast and slurred, and for a moment Yoninne thought he might strike her. "I have no choice now. We go to County Tsarang, just as you planned. Only now I know how I stand with you, and if we come out of this alive, I'll . . . I'll . . ." His voice choked off in anger and confusion, and he stomped out of the room.

For a long while after he left, Yoninne stared at the scarred wooden surface of the table. As if to blot out what had just happened, the details of her surroundings crowded into her consciousness: the fire crackling in the room's stove, the muted singing from downstairs, the dry, smoky smell of the place. She felt the tears building in her eyes, and tried to hold them back. She hadn't cried in fifteen years, and she'd be damned if she did now. But finally she couldn't help herself . . . perhaps she really was damned.

Fourteen

Bjault stared at the ceiling for several minutes before he realized he was awake, and that the pain in his guts was not cramps, but intense hunger. He slipped the quilt off his body and sat up. The wind howled from beyond the room's tiny chimney, and the torchlight from the hall flickered this way and that. He felt none of the dizziness and nausea of . . . the previous night? He glanced at his suit watch and saw that he had slept more than ten hours. The pain was gone now, and he felt as though he could go another century—if he didn't starve in the next ten minutes.

Bjault stood and pulled aside the door curtain. In the silverplate mirror above the washbasin, his brown face appeared gaunt and disheveled. He leaned close to the metal and pulled his lips away from his gums. For a long moment he stared at the bright blue line he saw running between teeth and gums. Lead poisoning: that blue stain was one of the few symptoms he remembered for it. Then the heavy metal concentration in

Azhiri foodstuffs must be hundreds of times higher than he had thought. And his recovery was at best a temporary thing. *How long do we really have? Weeks? Or only days?*

And if only days, should we stop eating? Or will starvation only speed the effects of the poisons already ingested?

But by the time he was dressed and walking down the hall to the dining room, Bjault had regained some of his good spirits. With luck, they might be back on Novamerika before he had another "attack." After all, Yoninne hadn't shown the faintest signs of discomfort yet. In many ways this world seemed to be doing her good: last night she had been positively solicitous.

He stepped through the curtains into the dining room, and saw the grim-faced group standing around the table. Two locals faced the Summerfolk. The Snowmen had slipped their parkas off, and stood naked from the waist up, their skin gleaming in the torchlight. One of them drew a triangular sheet of paper from his quilted leggings and said, "We've had another report from the Island Road, M'lords, since we first warned you of the storm. The way is still clear for about seven leagues, but the storm is moving toward us, and the transit lakes within it are freezing over too fast for our workers to keep them open. It may be a nineday before traffic can resume."

Pelio's voice was angry. "But we've *got* to move on. And our right of passage is guaranteed by treaty."

The Snowman's broad face clouded for a moment before he decided to laugh. "The treaty you made was with us, not with our weather. Feel free to travel the Island Road: six or seven jumps down the line you'll come out shattered across a three-foot thick layer of ice." His smile became a bit malevolent. "Are you really so anxious to escape from your own incredible bragging?" Apparently the story of Pelio's confrontation with his father at the Summer Festival had spread all the way to the Snowkingdom. There was a moment of dead silence as the prince's guards and officers tried to pretend they hadn't heard the Snowman's last remark. The wind sounded faintly through the stone walls.

Pelio did not respond to the gibe. "That's not what I meant. The treaty says Summerfolk have right of northern passage—even if you have to let us use another of your roads."

"Hmmph, I suppose if you insisted we'd have to let you take the North Road, though the rest of your kind seem content to stay here in Grechper and sit out the storm."

"We do insist," said Pelio.

"Very well." The other shrugged. "I'll get you a clearance." The Snowmen hiked their parkas back onto their torsos, and buttoned up. They turned and went down the stairs without any show of courtesy.

For a moment, no one spoke. Ajão sidled around the table to where breaded meats were piled high on a wooden plate. He was so hungry that this crisis took second place. He ate two of the meat-filled rolls and still the silence was unbroken. Ajão looked back and forth across the room, trying to figure out whether he was missing something: Pelio and Leg-Wot stood on opposite sides of the table, grimly avoiding each other's eyes.

Finally Pelio turned to their pilot-navigator. "Well?"

The army man came briefly to attention before answering. "They are as arrogant as usual, Your Highness, but I am afraid they are telling the truth. I seng surface ice on the transit lakes down the road. If we wait out the storm, we might be here three or four days."

"Captain, you know that we can't delay eighteen hours, much less three days." Shozheru's advisers had been adamant: the witlings were given just nine days to carry out their scheme. Of those nine, little more than one remained. "What about the North Road? The Snowmen said we could get clearance to travel that."

The soldier nodded and beckoned to a subordinate. The aide opened a leather case and rolled a world map onto the table. "Here we are at Grechper." The navigator pointed at a spot about halfway out from the pole. "Now if we could continue on our way down the Island Road"—he sketched a straight line across the disk to the far margin—"we would wind up in County Tsarang in about another eighty leagues—less than ten hours, if we pushed it. But if that way is closed to us we could use the North Road." He indicated a fine row of red dots that marched inward across the map to the pole. "We'll have to take on a local pilot, though, since I can't seng that route; they don't allow Summerfolk pilgrims much north of Grechper. It's about forty jumps to the North Pole. That's more than you might expect, but we can't afford quite as great a jolt on each jump as on Summer roads. The Snowmen's northern lakes are small and there's often ice in 'em—which could hull the yacht if we slammed in too hard.

"At the pole we switch to this road"—he pointed—"and start south for County Tsarang. That's another seventy-five hops."

The prince grimaced. "Altogether, that's thirty-five jumps further than the Island Road. How long will it take?"

"By the treaty, they need supply us with only one pilot, so I doubt if we'll do better than six jumps an hour . . . say twenty hours in all."

"Very well. We'll return to the yacht and prepare to leave.

At the same time, I want you"—Pelio was speaking to the consul now—"to do everything in your power to encourage prompt Snowman cooperation: we need that clearance for the North Road and we need a pilot who knows the way."

The elderly official bobbed his head. "As you will, Your Highness."

———

It took nearly three hours for the Snowmen to produce a qualified pilot. During most of that time, Ajão and the others huddled near their boat's tiny stoves and tried to keep warm. The skies were still clear and both moons were up now, at opposite ends of the sky—one full and the other a narrow cresent. To the southeast—beyond the shelves of frozen ocean—the stars disappeared a few degrees above the horizon. Along the edge of the lake, Snowmen chipped industriously at the smoky ice that formed even in the doped water. Only an occasional boat jumped into or out of the lake. At least fifty boats, more than half of them of the heavy Snowman design, were tied up at the wharves—all waiting for the Island Road to clear.

Toward noon, twilight brightened the southern sky as the sun made a valiant effort to pop above the horizon. But they were above the arctic circle here at Grechper, and the effort was in vain.

At one point, their navigator sent a message ball down the Island Road to the first transit lake that he senged to be ice-covered. Minutes later a reply smashed into the water near the yacht. The badly crushed wood ball was hauled aboard, and cut apart. The message within reported that the storm was furious and worsening.

And all that morning there on the frigid deck, Pelio and

Leg-Wot exchanged scarcely a word. The only time Ajão saw one look at the other was once when he caught Leg-Wot glaring at Pelio's back. Neither of them even asked him about his recovery. It was as if they were different people now; what happened while he was sleeping? He tried to get Yoninne into a private conversation, but she refused to be maneuvered.

Finally their new pilot—escorted by the two Snowmen who had originally brought the bad news about the storm—came stomping up the gangplank. Once aboard, the stalling—if that was what it had been—ended. The yacht's chief navigator took the fellow on a short tour of the hull, carefully pointing out the dimensions and weaknesses of its structure. Five minutes later they were renging steadily northward. The boat slid sideways in the water as it came out of each jump. Twilight faded quickly from the south. The moons looked down from a star-filled sky.

Ajão saw no more boats with the sun-over-fields seal of the Summerkingdom. The traffic along this road belonged to the Snowfolk: their boats, almost perfectly spheroidal, were unmistakable. The buildings around the shores were smaller now, and there were rarely towns beyond them. They looked to be little more than huts built from thick ice blocks. This far north, ground temperatures never rose above zero, even in the middle of summer; ice and snow were as good construction materials as any. Besides, the bedrock hereabouts was probably buried under several hundred meters of ice. League after league, the land remained a sterile, frigid desert. He realized now that even the Snowfolk couldn't maintain their way of life above the fiftieth parallel. No doubt the only people living by these lakes were the snow-chippers needed to keep the road open.

At one point the wind died—perhaps they were in the lee

of some mountain range hidden by the night. While their Snowman pilot took a rest, the crew inspected the boat's hull, and tried to chip away some of the greenish ice that covered the lower window slats. In the relative silence, the deck stoves crackled and spat. With the wind down, those stoves had a chance to heat the deck, and the men huddled near them. Ajão wondered that this sudden warmth didn't bring Samadhom out of whatever cubbyhole Pelio had found for him in the boat's hold.

Ajão looked through the ice-stained windows at a boat across the lake. Something new and curious was going on there: the craft slowly turned upside down, like a whale doing a lazy bellyroll. It started to roll back, then abruptly was teleported from the lake. Now why in heaven's name had the Snowmen rolled their boat before they jumped? He walked across the frosted deck to where Pelio stood warming himself. The prince didn't look up as Bjault asked about what he had seen in the water. For a moment he thought Pelio wasn't going to reply. Finally, the Azhiri shrugged. "I thought you and Ionina knew all the answers, Adgao," he said softly. "I'm an ignorant lout it suits you to use just now, remember?"

The light dawned on Bjault. He glanced across the deck at Yoninne, but that worthy stared grimly at the shoreline, determined to ignore them. *Well*, Bjault sighed to himself, *I suppose neither of us were meant to be intriguers*. He was almost relieved that the boy understood the situation. Aloud, he said, "There are many things we don't know, Your Highness. Perhaps that's why we . . . tricked you. If you were lost hundreds of leagues from home and surrounded by strangers who might be hostile, wouldn't you act a little bit, uh, sneaky—even toward the people you thought were friendly?"

The prince's gaze fell back to the fire shining through the

isinglass grating of the stove. "I suppose. From you I could accept this, but I thought Io—" He broke off, started on an entirely new course. "The boat you saw roll over was preparing to jump to some road in the southern hemisphere."

It was an ironic fact that in some situations the Azhiri could jump thousands of kilometers easier than hundreds: for if your destination lay due south as far below the equator as you were above it, then you could teleport there without suffering even the smallest jolt. So the Snowkingdom could occupy opposite ends of the world, yet—in a sense—still be a single, connected domain.

But that didn't really answer Bjault's question. "I mean, why do they turn the boat upside down?"

Pelio shrugged again. "The people at the South Pole are standing on their heads compared to us and no one can reng a boat unless it's first turned so the keel will point down at the destination. That's true even for the jumps we've been making, though you probably haven't noticed the trim changes, they were so slight."

This sounded like nonsense, till Ajão saw that it could follow from conservation of energy: if no adjustments were necessary, you might make a perpetual-motion machine by teleporting a pendulum back and forth between the North and South poles. An interesting and curious fact—but now he could think of nothing more to ask. And it seemed that Pelio had nothing more to say. Despite all the men on the deck, the boy was completely, miserably alone. Ajão sighed and returned to his seat.

Their arrival at the North Pole was unexpected and abrupt. Suddenly they were floating in a new lake, several times larger than previous ones. The traffic was heavy here—as if this lake were the juncture of many routes. Ice-block warehouses stood all around the water, many connected by hallways whose roofs barely poked above the dustlike snow that blew across the water from the plain beyond. If those dumpy buildings were the palace they'd been hearing about, then this was quite an anticlimax.

But Pelio pointed at the horizon. In the middle distance Ajão saw a collection of low domes and stubby towers, all gleaming silver-blue in the moonlight. Here and there, tiny holes broke the smooth curves. At Ajão's gentle but persistent prodding, Pelio explained: "Those are windows; the watch-towers are two hundred feet tall. In a way, the Snowfolk palace is even more secure than my father's Keep. At both poles the palace is surrounded by hundreds of miles of ice. Any pilgrims who make it this far would be seen from those towers long before they get to the palace."

Sixty meters high, thought Bjault in amazement; the figure put the palace in a new perspective. Someone must know some statics to build with ice on that scale. The palace was in a class apart from the shabby snow huts they had seen along the road.

Their Snowman pilot forced open a hatch and leaned out to shout through the wind at the masked and muffled figures on the wharf below. The two on the wharf listened a moment, then waved and trudged slowly back to their shelter. The pilot shut the hatch and the torrent of frigid air sweeping the deck became a mere breezy draft.

"We're getting permission to enter the transit lake within the palace," said Pelio. "It will be easier to check the hull and clean the windows in there. . . . This is more courtesy than I had expected."

Twin yellow lights glowed from one of the dark holes in a palace tower. The pilot looked at the lights, nodded, and sat down. For just a moment he concentrated on this last jump, and then they were within the Snowpalace. The vast room would have been completely dark but for the blades of moonlight that speared down through slits in the dome above them. They were floating in a pool some fifty meters across. Just beyond the water, a ring of pillars—each as wide as the pool itself—tapered up toward the roof. Yet for all their apparent strength, those columns stood translucent in the pale moonlight, their knifelike corners transparent. Several crewmen eased open the main hatch, and now Ajão could see that the floor beyond the pool was littered with ice or snow—a strange messiness, considering the geometric perfection of everything else. But the air coming through the hatchway was warmer than outside the palace, and—most important—there was no wind.

Then the men by the opening slid slowly to their knees, and fell onto the outer deck. Pelio stood up, started toward the fallen men, but the chief navigator waved the witlings back as he and his crew ran toward the still figures. Bjault felt Leg-Wot's hand close painfully around his elbow, heard her whisper, "Gas!" in Homespeech. And the moment she said it, he knew she must be right. He had participated in enough space-emergency drills to recognize this type of casualty.

By now, most of the crew were clustered around the fallen men. "Do you suppose they were kenged, Captain?" one of them shouted at the chief navigator.

The navigator shook his head angrily. "You didn't sense an attack, did you? Besides, the Snowman's down, too." And as he spoke his knees gave way and he pitched heavily forward, across the other bodies. Around him there were cries of terror, quickly turning into choking sounds as the others collapsed. The two Novamerikans held their breath as the crewmen fell, first the ones by the door and then those further and further away. Finally, only Leg-Wot and Bjault were left standing. They stared silently, helplessly at each other. They knew what was happening, but there was nothing they could do about it.

At last Ajão had to inhale. He smelled nothing—no corrosive taint, anyway. But suddenly he was on his knees, and reality was slipping away. Somewhere far away, he heard Leg-Wot swearing to herself, as she, too, accepted the inevitable.

Fifteen

aylight. It was the first thing Leg-Wot sensed as she struggled back toward consciousness: a cheerful yellow glow that penetrated her eyelids and made her think of spring mornings on Homeworld. But her fingers were numb and her back cramped with cold. Where was she? Her eyes opened and she stared up into the sparkling glints of sunlight coming off the icy pillars and roof above her—the Snow-palace! They were still trapped in the Snowpalace. Only now the sun was up, high enough in the sky so that its light fell directly on the glazed floor, and glittered off the edges and facets of the dome's supporting pillars. But this was impossible! The sun wouldn't rise over the Snowpalace till spring.

Someone groaned nearby. Yoninne forced herself to a sitting position and looked across the heap of dyed animal furs she sat upon. There were Pelio and Bjault. Pelio looked as though he had been awake for several minutes. Yoninne turned quickly away from him. It was Ajão who had groaned: he was just coming to. She crawled across the furs to him.

"The light. Where did all the light come from?" she asked.

Pelio pursed his lips but said nothing. Bjault spoke weakly, "Looks as though they've jumped us to the South Pole."

They? Leg-Wot turned to follow his gaze. "They" were Snowmen. A large party of servant and soldier types stood in the middle distance, while just ten meters away, five others—all dressed in heavily jeweled leggings—sat around a fur-covered table. She recognized at least one of those: the greasy character she had met in the Summerpalace—Bre'en, was that his name? Even now that the witlings were awake, their captors regarded them impassively, as if the prisoners were insects on display. Beside the table stood the black hull of the ablation skiff that she and Ajão had so carefully stowed in the hold of Pelio's yacht. And there, on the table, sat the maser, the machine pistols—even the machete from their survival kit! The witlings had been so sure that only a Guildsman or a high nobleman of Summer could rob the Keep that they had walked unknowingly into the hands of the real enemy.

The Bre'en creature stood up, his naked chest gleaming in the yellow sunlight. "Good, you are awake." His face creased with the same easy grin he had displayed back in the Summerpalace. "Ionina, Adgao, I regret that we used trickery to bring you here to the pole. There is no storm on the Island Road. But don't blame your men for not senging our deception; the road is indeed frozen over—we gave our ice-chipping crews a few hours' vacation and the winter cold did the rest.

"Frankly, our lies were born of desperation. You were too well guarded and too misinformed for us to approach you directly. Yet, as evidence of our good intentions, you have the honor of being interviewed by the king of our land and his highest ministers." Bre'en bowed toward the short and exceptionally fat Snowman who sat at the head of the table. That worthy raised his round chin a fraction of a degree to acknowledge the introduction. The guards behind the five stared impassively.

Before the Snowman could continue, Ajão interrupted. "How did you, how did you—"

"How did we render you senseless? We of the poles have our magics, too, Adgao, although they do not compare with what we have seen of yours. In certain places in the North, during the winter there, it becomes so cold that thin layers of a magical snow grow on the ice—a secret gift of nature to our kingdom. This enchanted snow disappears when warmed, yet if it is warmed in an enclosed space, then anyone living in that space must fall to sleep."

Bull! thought Leg-Wot, as she tore the superstitious wrappings from the Snowman's statement. He must be talking about frozen CO_2. There might just be places cold enough on Giri for the stuff to form.

"In due time we will revive your crew." He waved at the transit pool behind him. Pelio's yacht floated near the far end, the hull tilting at an unnatural angle against the pool's wall. The boat's hatches were sealed. "But for now they are better off asleep."

Pelio shot to his feet. "You" (unknown word) "liar! You've killed my men." His glare turned upon the Snowking. "How dare you allow such treachery, Tru'ud? Do treaties mean so little to you?"

King Tru'ud started to sneer, then controlled himself and simply looked away from the prince. Bre'en was a good deal less cordial when he responded to the boy. "You are impertinent, Prince Pelio. No one has been murdered. We used the least force possible — and that only when it became clear that the Summerkingdom did not intend to share our visitors' knowledge. If we *had* killed your crew, why would we spare you? With your suspicions unspoken wouldn't it be easier to win over your two friends?"

The argument didn't appeal to Pelio. "I don't know why you didn't finish me off with the others. But I *do* know you can never let us go. Only as long as you can tell my family that a 'terrible accident' destroyed my yacht will you have any chance of avoiding war with the Summerkingdom."

Bre'en shrugged, and turned to the Novamerikans with an apologetic smile. "Anyway, we hope you will see the truth of what we say. At the Summerfest you claimed that you were somehow going to travel across the Great Ocean. We aren't sure if you were bluffing or not, but we do know that King Shozheru gave you only a few days to prepare for the attempt, and that he had secret plans to betray you in case you seemed close to success. You will find my king more lenient. He is prepared to give you protection, time, and personal comfort . . . if you will share your magic with us.

"And we know that magic is powerful, perhaps more powerful than the Guild itself. We had men in the hills north of Bodgaru at the time of your capture. One saw the flying monster come to your aid, and others saw it burning down through the sky, hundreds of miles north of you; the creature was making better time than most road boats do in those latitudes. We believe that if you had not been completely ignorant of the Talent, you might have succeeded in fighting off the troops that Prefect Moragha sent against you.

"Since that time, several of your talismans have come into our possession, and these further strengthened our notion of your importance." He gestured at the maser and other pieces of equipment that had been stolen from the Summerpalace.

"Yes," interrupted Pelio, "just how did you get these things out of the Keep?"

"That, of course, is our secret," said the Snowman. Then his egotism got the better of him and he grinned at Pelio. "But I can say that we did it even as you and Ionina looked on."

How was that possible? When she saw Bre'en and his men at the Keep, they had been empty-handed. The maser and the pistols were not large—none measured more than eighty by twenty centimeters—but you could hardly conceal them in your leggings. *Or could you?* Suddenly she remembered the strange, stiff-legged gait of Bre'en's servants, and a ghastly thought occurred to her; what if those men were amputees? If they could fool the guards' density sense . . . each stolen object could fit easily within the stubby outline of an Azhiri's lower leg. Of course, the men would be crippled for the rest of their lives, but that might not bother the Snowking. It was obvious he played rough.

"As I was saying," Bre'en resumed, "these devices only increased our respect for you. We lost two good men learning that this"—he pointed at one of the machine pistols—"rengs metal pebbles as fast-moving as anything our soldiers can reng. With this weapon, an untraveled recruit can be as deadly as a trooper who has spent years on pilgrimage." *Ah, the armies you could raise, eh, Bre'en?* thought Leg-Wot.

The Snowman reached across the table to touch the maser. "And this device proved almost as deadly. One of our men looked down the glassy end, while turning these knobs. He died in seconds, almost as though he had been kenged—yet the fellow was alert and fully Talented."

Bjault's voice was hesitant. "What exactly do you want from us?"

"The secret of your magic. Failing that, we want you to build us more of these things. We'd like to catch some of those sky monsters, too. In return you will have our assistance in your efforts to travel across the sea. Or, if you decide to remain in our kingdom permanently, we will offer you an honored place in our peerage."

Ajão nodded, and Leg-Wot wondered angrily if the old man really bought such promises. "May I talk with Yoninne?" he asked.

Pelio growled a curse under his breath.

"Certainly," said Bre'en, but the Snowman made no move to give them privacy.

Leg-Wot looked across the piled furs. "Well?" she said in Homespeech.

"Well," said Ajão in the same language, his voice as tremulous as before, "we're going to have to make this quick. Pelio's right; they murdered the crew. You just don't suffocate people with CO_2 and then leave them 'asleep' until you need them. You either revive them immediately or else they die."

Samadhom, poor Samadhom. It wasn't right, but somehow the tubby watchbear's death hurt the most.

"These are clever people, Yoninne. I think they revived Pelio just so they could make the points they did. Tru'ud's court has the taint of a 'modern' dictatorship—like we had at the end of the Interregnum. Those servants—no, don't turn to look; Bre'en and the others don't understand our language but they might be able to read your face—those servants are alike enough to be brothers. I wouldn't be surprised if the Snowking breeds witlings like cattle.

"I suspect Tru'ud will eliminate us the moment he thinks

we've given him a decisive advantage over his enemies—though we'll die of metallic poisoning long before that happens."

Perhaps Bjault wasn't quite the ivory-tower man he seemed. "Well then, damn it, what are we going to do?" Out of the corner of her eye she saw that the Snowmen were becoming restless.

"I . . . I don't know, Yoninne," he said and Leg-Wot knew that here, at least, the indecision in his voice was real. "It looks as though we'll have to play along—for the moment."

"Hmf." Yoninne turned back to the Snowking and his ministers. "We will cooperate, but Prince Pelio must not be harmed," she said in Azhiri.

Bre'en nodded, and Pelio's expression froze in an implacable glare. *I'm so sorry, Pelio*, the thought came unexpectedly into her mind. She was still selling him out, even though she had secured him—temporary—safety.

Bre'en was all smiles now, and even Tru'ud's grim face seemed to hold a bit of triumph. "What you ask is only what we intended," said the Snowman diplomat. "Your quarters have already been prepared and heated to the temperature Summerfolk find comfortable."

Yoninne felt unwilling gratitude at this. Her body ached from the constant cold, and her sweat-soaked parka was like a clammy hand on her skin. A room temperature around freezing might be pleasant indoor warmth for Bre'en, but it was hideously uncomfortable for the likes of Pelio and Yoninne Leg-Wot—and it was probably hell for Bjault.

The three witlings stood, painfully aware of the cramps in their muscles. As they walked slowly down over the piled furs, Snowman troopers closed in around Ajão and

Yoninne. Behind them, Pelio followed without so much as a single guard. *It's Ajão and me they fear*, thought Leg-Wot. The two Novamerikans were wizards who must be carefully watched, especially when they came near their magical gadgets. Pelio, on the other hand, was less than no threat to the Snowmen.

Tru'ud grunted something at Bre'en in the glottalized Snowman language; the diplomat walked around the table to the ablation skiff. "His Majesty is curious about this object. Since it's off your yacht, we haven't had a chance to examine it. It's certainly the largest thing of yours we've seen; is it some kind of vehicle? A self-renging boat perhaps?" The Snowman pulled at the skiff's circular hatch, which already stood ajar. The black ceramic port slid easily back and—

—Samadhom poked his furry muzzle over the lip of the entrance. *Meep?* he inquired curiously of the dumfounded Snowman. So that was where the animal had been holed up! Pelio had put him into what was probably the best-insulated volume on the whole road boat—their own ablation skiff!

For just an instant, everyone stood frozen. Pelio was the first to recover, and what he did was as much a surprise as Samadhom's sudden appearance. In a single motion he vaulted across the table, snatching up the short machete the Snowmen had stolen from the Novamerikans' survival kit. Pelio twisted around as he landed, pulled Tru'ud off his seat, and slid the razor-sharp blade against the Snowman's throat.

"Stand back—back!" Tru'ud pitched against him and a thin line of red appeared across the king's throat. For a moment Tru'ud's men glared silently at the prince. Pelio's face turned pale and Yoninne realized that the Snowmen had tried to scramble his insides. But Samadhom was protecting him— just as Yoninne had been protected when King Shozheru had attacked her.

She stepped quickly to the table, and swept up the maser. The needle on its power supply rested dead on zero. No matter. She turned and leveled the stubby tube at her erstwhile guards. "You heard Prince Pelio. Move." The men slowly obeyed. Leg-Wot glanced at Tru'ud's advisers by the far end of the table. "And you people. Stay away from those." She waved the maser at the machine pistols.

As Bjault retrieved the weapons, Pelio relaxed his hold on Tru'ud a fraction and gave Yoninne a triumphant, mocking smile. "I guessed you two would fly whichever way the wind was blowing," he said.

What could she say to that?

Ajão peered into the magazines of the two pistols. "One's empty and the other is hopelessly jammed," he said in Homespeech.

"The maser's dead, too," Yoninne replied in the same language. "But they don't know that."

"Well?" Pelio broke in angrily. "Do we return to our original plan? There's no other choice now, you know."

Yoninne nodded. Death might be seconds away, but somehow she was happier now than before—when life had depended on sucking up to the Snowmen; now it depended on fighting them. "But how?"

Pelio looked over his shoulder at a craft in the transit pool. "We'll take that speedboat," he said abruptly, carelessly. Tru'ud twisted in his grip and Pelio bore down slightly with the machete. "We'll go all the way to County Tsarang—with Tru'ud as our hostage!"

It was an insane plan, thought Leg-Wot. They were thousands of kilometers inside Snowman territory; any road they followed could be blocked by whole armies. Then she looked around the vast hall. Everyone—the servants, the troops, the advisers—stared in horror at the knife held on Tru'ud's throat. Perhaps this dictatorship was not quite as modern as Bjault thought. She guessed the Snowmen would do anything in exchange for their king's safety. Besides—as her father had often said—it's far better to act on a bad plan than to wait for a good one to come along.

She turned to Bre'en. "All right, Snowman. We want passage north. Put that"—she waved at the skiff—"aboard the boat there, and give us a pilot who can navigate to County Tsarang."

Bre'en spread his hands. Of all those present, he seemed the only one who had recovered his composure. "Such men are rare. Besides myself, I know of no one in the palace who could take you as far as the county's border. You could, of course, change pilots along the way . . . Or you could reconsider. We still bear *you* no ill feeling."

Leg-Wot smelled a rat. Changing pilots en route would be an invitation to disaster. And the alternative—taking Bre'en along with them—was almost as bad. The man was slippery.

"Why would you, of all people, know the way?" she asked.

The Snowman seemed almost relaxed now. He ignored the supposedly deadly maser pointed at his thick waist. "As a young man, I served in His Majesty's army. I worked with Desertfolk between here and County Tsarang. I learned every road I could, so I wouldn't have to depend on always having the right pilot available. Of course, most officers wouldn't take the trouble, but I—"

"Be quiet, both of you," said Pelio. "You'll pilot us to County Tsarang, Bre'en. But if you're lying about your skill—" He pulled back hard on Tru'ud, half choking the man.

Ajão seemed on the point of raising some further objection, but Pelio silenced the archaeologist with a look. It was going to be hard to make even the most reasonable suggestions to the prince from now on. "Samadhom. Here!" Pelio called the watchbear out of the skiff. The animal landed heavily on the fur carpet and padded slowly across to his master's feet.

Bre'en shook his head in wonder as his eyes followed Sam across the floor. "An amazing animal!" His tone was almost conversational. "He's protecting all three of you at once. We have no watchbears that Talented." Yoninne looked out at the pale, staring faces. Witling slaves aside, anyone in that crowd could kill her and Pelio and Ajão in a fraction of a second—if it weren't for Samadhom. And if it weren't for the knife at Tru'ud's throat, that crowd could beat them to death in scarcely more time. Bre'en must have read the expression on her face. "Without great good luck," he said, "you would not now be alive. Such luck can't hold, you—"

"I said to be quiet," Pelio repeated, and Bre'en fell silent. "Get the magicians' sphere onto yonder speedboat. . . . Quickly!"

King Tru'ud gargled apoplectically, and in his rage admitted what the witlings had guessed: "You three . . . never will live for this." The words were jumbled, both by anger and Tru'ud's unfamiliarity with the language of the Summerkingdom. "Your death will be pain, much more pain than we gave your crew to die."

Sixteen

League after league, Bre'en teleported the witlings and
King Tru'ud northward, yet only the service buildings
around the transit lakes seemed to change. Beyond their tiny
boat's windows, the sky remained a deep, cloudless blue.
From thirty degrees off the glare-white horizon, the sun cast
long, bluish shadows across the jumbled madness of the
antarctic ice. It was way too bright to look at, though
Yoninne's wrist chron said it was early morning, Summerkingdom time. Here the night was more than one hundred
days away.

For the moment, the Snowking's forces were letting them
proceed toward County Tsarang. If they could make it to
that vassal state of Summer, they might yet have a chance to
carry out the scheme that had once seemed the most dangerous part of Ajão's plan, the scheme that would take them to
Draere's Island.

The boat they had stolen was small and its hull was strong,

strong enough so they could safely skip every other transit lake along the road. They were making good progress even though they rested five or ten minutes between each jump: time for Bre'en to prepare for the next hop, time for Pelio to check the harnesses that bound the two hostages.

"I'm not taking any chances with our friends," said Pelio. "No matter how highly trained, they can't reng away from us as long as they're tied down."

Ajão said something about molecular bonding energies, but Leg-Wot already understood what Pelio meant: when Azhiri teleported, they took at least part of their surroundings with them; only Guildsmen had perfect control of the volume renged. In order to teleport themselves from the boat, Tru'ud and Bre'en would have to cut through the straps that held them—an act that was far beyond the power of the Talent. Yoninne looked at Pelio with new respect. The trick was one that she—and perhaps Ajão—would not have thought of. For that matter, they wouldn't be heading north right now if it weren't for Pelio's guts and initiative. Was it simply desperation that drove him, or had he been a man all along—all the time she treated him like a weak-willed adolescent?

"I think we're being paced," Ajão said abruptly, two jumps later.

"What?" said Pelio.

"Look around the lake. Several of those boats are awfully familiar."

"Yes," the prince said slowly. "And every lake is a bit more crowded than the last. I'll wager the Snowmen messaged ahead, calling up every available army boat. In effect, we're as tightly surrounded as we were back in their palace." He grinned at Bre'en and Tru'ud. "But it won't do you any good.

If they blast our boat, you'll go down with it." When the Snowmen did not respond he went on. "In a way I should be grateful to you two. You've given me a chance to prove I'm not completely helpless."

"You needed the watchbear," Bre'en pointed out glumly.

"That's true. But you practically died of shock when I jumped Tru'ud. Witlings just don't attack normal people; we're less than animals to you. You couldn't conceive that I'd be a threat, so you didn't put even a single guard on me. And for once, I was able to take advantage of that arrogance."

Bre'en didn't reply, but Tru'ud shouted wildly in his native language. Pelio just smiled.

In two hours they made seventeen jumps and covered about four thousand kilometers, moving all the way to the Antarctic Circle. The sun edged down toward the southeast, and its light turned the snows into sparkling gold. More and more they saw bedrock jut up through the yellow-white, and quick-flowing streams pouring from the ice and slush into over-full transit lakes. Another four hops, and the snow was mostly gone. A tundra extended off to the horizon—and she saw green out there! But the next jump brought even greater change: the squalid stone buildings around the lake were themselves surrounded by a maze of tents and hundreds of busy Snowfolk. Beyond the strangely checkered tents she glimpsed herds of hairy, four-footed animals grazing off the summer vegetation. So that was how the Snowfolk supported themselves. They were nomads on the grandest scale; they must reng their herds from pole to pole, as the seasons brought a little vegetation first to the North and then to the South. No wonder their cities at the other end of the world had seemed so drab and empty.

Her view of the surrounding countryside was cut off as one of the pursuing army boats splashed into the lake. Their unwelcome companions numbered more than twenty now; God only knew what other forces were pacing them in the lakes ahead and behind. Yet it was still a stalemate: the Snowmen had their army, and the witlings had the Snowking.

Somewhere in the next two jumps, the sun slid behind the horizon. As twilight deepened, the air became steadily warmer. The witlings doused the boat's tiny stove, and—several leagues further north—shed their heavy clothing. While she covered Bre'en and Tru'ud with the supposedly lethal maser, Pelio loosened the Snowmen's restraints so they could remove their parkas and over-leggings. Leg-Wot almost felt sorry for their two prisoners. They had been strapped down for hours now. Tru'ud squirmed uncomfortably after each jump, and Bre'en seemed to be tiring—at least, Pelio allowed him a longer rest between jumps.

For more than an hour they drove on through darkness, with only the stars above, and the campfires ashore, to see by—just enough light to make out their ominous entourage. And then, fantastically, twilight returned to the east: their path had taken them from the antarctic day through a narrow sliver of lower-latitude night, and now the sun was about to pop back up again. The land revealed by the new twilight was far different from what they had seen before. The tents and the grazing animals were gone. Dry and rocky desolation had replaced them. The buildings surrounding the lake were smooth, almost streamlined—adobe? Scrub brush scraggled around the water's edge, where dark-skinned men stood silently watching.

"Those are Desertfolk ashore," said Pelio. "We're in their domain now—but it will make little difference to us. Wherever Summer lands adjoin desert, these people harass us.

Their lords are all allied with the Snowking, so we are in as much danger here as before. The most we can hope is that Tru'ud's army will be slowed a bit trying to coordinate with the local warlords. I think—"

Yoninne wasn't looking at Tru'ud when he made his move, and for an instant everything was a confused jumble. The Snowman lunged across the boat's narrow deck, the straps of his harness flying loose around him. He slammed into the half-open hatch, and for a moment hung partway in, partway out, his enormous belly stuck in the opening. But before Pelio could get to him, Tru'ud heaved himself through and splashed heavily into the water below.

She whirled on Bre'en, brought her maser to bear. "Get your hands in the air!" The Snowman diplomat had twisted in his seat, his hands straining to within centimeters of an inconspicuous silver rivet on his harness. *Damnation, some kind of quick release latch.* So all Tru'ud's squirming had had a purpose. "You'll burn if you don't raise your hands," Yoninne said, and Bre'en's hands slowly retreated from the latch. Behind them, Samadhom *meeped* anxiously.

Pelio leaned out to look into the dark waters, then slammed the hatch shut and scrambled back into his harness. "Get us out of here, Bre'en, *now!*"

Apparently the Snowman saw sudden death in the other's eyes, for he obeyed immediately.

But Pelio hardly seemed to notice. "Tru'ud must have jumped to a different part of the transit lake the moment he hit the water. There was no way we could have picked him up. Now we're really in for it. It won't take the army more than a few minutes to discover their king has escaped us—and then having Bre'en hostage isn't going to do us any good. Do you hear that, Bre'en? You'll die with us unless you can keep away from the other boats."

For a moment Bre'en did not respond. In the transit lake the army boats were arriving. Finally he said, "You're probably right, Prince Pelio. Your crimes are so great that my king will no doubt pay any price to punish you." His gaze turned to Ajão and Yoninne. "But you two are still mere accomplices. And we need you as much as before—don't you see that guarantees your safety? You have the weapons; put the Summerboy in his place. Surrender."

Pelio turned to look at Yoninne, but he said nothing. *Most likely, Bre'en's promises are lies*, thought Leg-Wot, *but what choice do we have . . . ?* "No!" she said abruptly, without looking to see if Bjault agreed. She wasn't going to sell Pelio out again. "You just keep renging this boat north, Snowman."

Bre'en glared at her, but obeyed. The next lake was much the same as the one they had left—an oasis set in twilit desert. Seconds later, the army boats splashed in around them. Pelio looked at her the way she had missed so much since Grechper. "What are we going to do, Ionina? The only places Bre'en can take us are under Tru'ud's control. No matter where we go, they'll sink us."

Before she could answer, the early-morning silence was broken by a splintering crash from the east side of the hull. Thunder ripped back into the sky from the point of impact. Shards of hardwood fell into the boat's interior and Samadhom keened in pain. Yoninne twisted in her seat: it looked as if some blunt object had smashed against the upper hull, punching an irregular hole. Through the maze of shattered quartz and tangled wood she saw the Snowman boats resting in the water just thirty meters away. The Snowmen were renging air from half a world away, air moving hundreds of meters per second relative to their boat. In the space of just two seconds, the attackers struck three more times, breaching the hull all the way to the waterline. Then Bre'en jumped the tiny speedboat and suddenly the morning was still again.

Samadhom! Leg-Wot strained in her harness to get a closer look at the watchbear. A ten-centimeter sliver of wood protruded from the animal's furry shoulder, and that fur was slowly turning red. His deep green eyes showed wide borders of white as he tried to lick the wound. Yet he couldn't be too badly hurt—otherwise Bre'en would have killed them all by now. She started to pry open the buckles on her harness—Sam should be moved away from the crumbling bulkhead—but just then five army boats splashed into the oasis' dark waters.

Two gouts of water—accompanied by characteristic thunder—fountained from the lake's surface. Then the enemy got their range and the hypervelocity bolts of wind slammed into the speedboat's hull, shredding it still further. "They're being gentle," Bre'en shouted over the sounds of destruction. He looked haggard and scared now, his oily manner gone. "They could reng water at us, or even rocks."

"Jump, damn you, jump!" Leg-Wot screamed in Home-speech, but the other got her meaning. They jumped and Leg-Wot felt herself lurch upward against the restraining straps: they had hopped east rather than north. They were no longer moving to get somewhere, but only to avoid the enemy. It was a futile effort: the new lake was already occupied. Blow after blow broke across the boat. The deck tilted toward the gaping vents at the waterline.

"We're boxed in," Pelio said to no one in particular. "They must have boats on every transit lake for leagues. Wherever we go, they'll keep hitting us." *Crunch.* Slivers of

wood flew up from the deck and the boat slid sideways into the water. The enemy boats were moving in now, as if this were a delicate operation they must do piece by piece; so they meant to save Bre'en after all. She saw the Snowman's hands edging toward the quick release on his harness, and waved her maser at him. If he escaped, the enemy could dispense with delicacy.

But even as their speedboat was being hacked from under them, old Bjault piped up with an inane question. "You said you learned to seng this part of the world because you were a soldier?" he said to Bre'en. Leg-Wot didn't know whether to laugh or swear: was Bjault so far out of touch, he didn't see the end was seconds away?

Bre'en just grunted in response. "Well, then," continued Ajão, "you must have learned to seng spots much smaller than transit lakes. You must know all sorts of hidden—"

"Of course!" shouted Pelio over the crashing wind. "Ambush points, food caches! You can take us to hundreds of places these people won't find for hours."

In the brightening twilight, the hate in Bre'en's face was plain to see. "No!" he shrilled. *He came so close*, thought Yoninne, *to saving his own neck and recapturing us, too*. She turned the maser's blunt muzzle on him, and tried to ignore the water rising about her ankles. "One more jump, Bre'en. Take us somewhere no one has been in a long time."

Seventeen

J *ump.* A groaning, ripping sound came through the speedboat's belly. The deck split down the middle and Yoninne was looking straight up into the morning sky— then down at the water. Around her timbers and planking flew in all directions. Finally she came to rest, hanging upside down from her harness. For a moment she swung gently back and forth on the straps. All was silent except for a faint *drip drip drip* somewhere behind her. From the marshy ground a meter below her head, scraggly brush thrust stiff fingers within ten centimeters of her face, bringing an odor of muck and decay.

Yoninne pulled the harness release and the universe spun around her as she swung down onto the boggy ground. She staggered to her feet and walked dazedly around the wreckage.

Dawn had come to the desert: peeking over the jumbled

plain to the east, the sun turned the rocks and sand to tan and orange, the brush to dusty green.

Very pretty. But the speedboat was an unrecognizable pile of junk. Bre'en had renged them into some kind of marsh. The boat had skidded out of the water and rolled across the ground to the marsh's edge, where it broke apart on jagged rocks. But the ablation skiff was undamaged. It had bounced clear of the wreckage to sit, a dull black sphere, in the brush surrounding the marsh.

There were voices now from within the wreckage, and she thought she heard *meeping*, too. She poked around the split timbers that thrust deep through the brush into the marshy soil. "Ionina!" Pelio called. She found him under what was left of the boat's bottom plates. Except for the beginnings of a massive bruise along his jaw and neck, he looked okay. She clambered through the wreckage to reach him. Together they eased back the curved planking that pinned him to his couch. For an instant, Yoninne's hand rested on his arm, and they looked at each other silently. Then Pelio smiled at her—the first time in how many hours?—and they turned to recover the others.

In half an hour they were all sitting around the edge of the marsh, huddled down in the bushes. Considering the damage the boat had taken, they had come out awfully well. Bre'en had a broken ankle (which could only serve to make him more manageable), and Ajão had come through without even a bruise. Sam was a different story: the watchbear seemed alert and comfortable as he lay in the brush next to Pelio, but the fur across his shoulder was matted with blood. . . .

The sun stood almost ten degrees above the horizon now, its glare blotting the eastern plains from view. The air turned dry and hot, and something—animals hidden in the rocks?—set up a terrible buzzing. What had—by contrast with the antarctic—seemed warm before, had been nothing but the chill of a desert night. By noon this place would be hotter than anything she'd seen in the Summerkingdom.

Bre'en looked sourly at the heat ripples rising over the brownish green marsh. Pelio had used one of the boat cables to tie the Snowman to the biggest, sturdiest bush in sight. Bre'en couldn't reng away from them, but he had what freedom of movement his broken ankle permitted. "So?" the haggard Bre'en said, grimacing at the pain that must be shooting up his leg. "At most you've gained yourselves an hour of freedom. Right now my king's army and their allies are checking every mudhole inside ten leagues. And the Desertfolk know these lands: to them water is terribly important. You'll be lucky to—"

"Oh? They know where every last drop of water is, eh?" Yoninne broke in nastily. "Then why don't your friends have a settlement here?"

Bre'en pointed at the circle of rocks that peeked through the scrub around the marsh. "Someone *was* here once; they even had a transit lake. If I remember right, there are ruins on the other side of the bog . . . buildings burned right down to their foundations."

"The water is so thoroughly poisoned that only scragweed can drink it," said Pelio sharply.

Bre'en nodded, almost smugly. "Some of my . . . some of the partisans were overeager on that score. They felt your Summerfolk were a bit discourteous, planting your towns in the margin of their desert."

Pelio started to reply, then waved angrily at their hostage. "You're wasting our time, Bre'en." He turned to Yoninne. "We've got to decide what to do. Should we hide out here, or take another chance with the Desertfolk's roads? Your strange sphere"—he gestured at the ablation skiff—"could hold us all, and it certainly seems sturdy enough to be used as a road boat."

"Could Bre'en jump us all the way into County Tsarang?"

The Snowman smiled crookedly and shook his head. "I doubt it," said Pelio, confirming Bre'en's wordless assertion. "The county has always been well guarded against unwelcome pilgrims. He could reng us to a border lake, but that's about all."

"Then I don't see what good it would do to get back on the road," Yoninne said glumly. "At least the Snowmen don't know where we are now."

Bjault broke the long silence that followed. "You said this was once a Summerfolk village, Bre'en. It must be close to land that's still under Summer control."

The Snowman tried to laugh but it was a hollow, croaking sound. "It is, you brown-faced fool, it is. County Tsarang lies just beyond those mountains." He waved toward the west. "It would be one quick jump if you had someone who could seng the way. But it's a death march if you try to walk it without water."

"Hmm," said Bjault, as if this were some very encouraging answer. The archaeologist rose stiffly and walked over to the skiff.

Pelio watched him for a moment, then said to Yoninne, "You told me once that yonder sphere can fly."

"Yes, but only downward, to slow a fall." She didn't try to explain the workings of the parachute. *Face it, girl: we're stuck.* Even if Bre'en were exaggerating—even if the walk to the mountains were a piece of cake—it still wouldn't do them any good. They needed the skiff, too. Without it, they couldn't carry out Ajão's plan for getting to the telemetry station on Draere's island.

As they talked, Bjault stood silently, looking first at the skiff and then at the ragged line of mountains to the west. Suddenly he shouted in Homespeech, "That's it! Look, Yoninne: we have a good parachute and we have Bre'en. We can teleport high-velocity air into the chute and lift ourselves right up by our bootstraps!" A grin split his dark face from ear to ear.

Leg-Wot realized her mouth was hanging open. Why, Bre'en could sail their skiff right over the mountains into County Tsarang. Suddenly she was on her feet, running through the brush to Ajão and the skiff. She pulled open the hatch, and clambered into the still-cool darkness. A loud *sprong* sounded as she pulled the chute release, and the olive-colored, fiberene parachute burst from the top of the skiff's heat-scarred hull. She grabbed a fold from the heavy pack and pulled streamer after streamer of gauzy fiberene onto the ground. Bjault tried ineffectually to help.

All the while, Pelio and Bre'en looked on with expressions of wonder and—in Bre'en's case—suspicion. Yoninne turned to them. "I was wrong, Pelio." She waved at the hundreds of square meters of olive chute spread across the rocks and bushes. "Using Bre'en's Talent, we *can* fly." She explained what the Snowman would have to do.

Thredegar Bre'en had risen to his knees to stare at them. He swayed slightly from side to side, and his face was filmed with sweat. But he seemed to understand what she wanted, even if he didn't see what the effect would be. Finally he said, "You've been working me for hours. How much longer do you think I can go on?"

She glanced at Pelio, saw that the prince couldn't tell if Bre'en were faking or not. Bre'en certainly hadn't been getting as much rest as their pilots had during the trip to the North

Pole. But had those rest-stops been a matter of comfort or necessity? Then she remembered the med-kit in the skiff. The kit contained booster drugs. Perhaps they wouldn't help—perhaps they would blot out what Talent the Snowman could still use—but the alternative was simply to threaten the fellow, and that ploy had already been used for all it was worth. She started toward the skiff's hatch and said to Bre'en, "I've got some, uh, potions here that should bring your strength back." She might as well *seem* confident, anyway.

For an instant she saw stark terror in the Snowman's face, and realized how thoroughly his people must respect the witlings' "magic." Bre'en's fear turned to dark anger, and the man straightened, his fatigue visibly diminished. What she had offered as help was actually the greatest threat she could have made.

"All right, then," Pelio said to Bre'en. "Let's get aboard."

Eighteen

Yoninne spent a few extra seconds outside the skiff, trying to spread the chute as far as possible across the thicketed ground. She worked with frantic haste, and tried to suppress the constant urge to look over her shoulder at the marsh. Now that they had a means of escaping, she expected their pursuers to come popping into existence at any moment.

At last she climbed into the dark interior of the skiff, leaving the hatch ajar. Things were even more crowded than when the powered sledge had been aboard. Samadhom, Bre'en, and the witlings shared the skiff with several tons of carefully seated lead ballast. They would need that ballast if they ever reached County Tsarang, but for now it only made their task more difficult. She settled into the webbed pilot's seat—left vacant for her by Ajão, who apparently realized she would need as much room as possible.

"Start off slowly, Bre'en. We don't know just how this will work."

The Snowman—crammed between herself and Pelio—didn't say anything, but the brush outside the hatch cracked and strained in a sudden gust of wind. Through the skiff's window slits, Yoninne saw the chute press itself against the ground. "Not that way," she said abruptly. "Reng in air from the northwest."

The breeze vanished for a moment, then returned. The olive fiberene floated upward as the air moved over it. In seconds, the canopy had bellied out before them, tugging the shrouds that extended horizontally from the top of the skiff. Pelio gasped as he looked through the narrow windows at the immense olive disk and finally realized just how it might be possible for them to fly. But the wind barely filled the chute; its lower edge still rested on the ground. Bre'en was probably stalling, but Leg-Wot did not object. They'd get their necks broken if they didn't handle this takeoff cautiously. "More," was all she said to their hostage.

The wind became a shrieking, pulsing hurricane, as the Snowman teleported gout after gout of air into the canopy. The shrouds bounced back and forth, absorbing the irregular thrust, and the skiff lurched forward with a whiplash, rocking motion. Something—a boulder?—crashed against the hull, sending them half a meter into the air. Bre'en's windstorm was dragging them across the jagged stones that surrounded the marsh. The skiff's interior became a jumble of randomly extended hands and feet as everyone—except Yoninne and Bre'en, who were strapped down—caromed wildly about. Leg-Wot pulled hard on the trim controls with little effect.

"Give us some up, or we'll all die," she screamed at the Snowman. "Jump the air in from further west," she added, jabbing him in the side. Bre'en got the message, for suddenly the chute swung twenty degrees into the air, and after one last bone-crunching collision, the skiff was—provisionally—airborne. The noise suddenly faded, though they were still being dragged along by Bre'en's wind storm: when Leg-Wot looked out the hatch she saw scrub and rocks streaming past just a couple of meters below. If they hit anything now, the hull would crack open. She worked at the chute's trim controls, trying to direct the thrust. The controls were manual, but well designed, and soon their climb angle was almost forty-five degrees. The ride was still bumpy—much like the antique pulse-jet her father once let her fly—but she had control and they were putting distance between themselves and the ground.

The thrust came ragged now; Bre'en lay gasping in his webbed seat. Leg-Wot touched his arm. "Rest for a moment."

The other nodded without looking up and the gale roaring around the skiff became more of a breeze. Yoninne pushed open the hatch and looked at the lands below. The skiff's altimeter said they were twenty-five hundred meters up. She could believe it: the ground looked soft—almost velvety—and the grazing sunlight sent long blue shadows across the hills. At their present sink rate, about eight meters per second, Bre'en could relax for a minute or so.

Behind them, a dusky green ring sat in the desert—the poisoned oasis they had just departed. But that marsh was no longer empty! An egg-shaped road boat had materialized at the center of the swamp. And she thought she could make out tiny figures standing in the dry brush at its margin.

Pelio leaned past Bre'en to look out the hatch. For a moment he just stared; then he laughed. "We're too far up. The fools can see us but they can't seng us. Safe. We're safe!" Suddenly he seemed to realize just how much sheer empty space separated them from the ground. He shivered, and carefully retreated from the opening.

One thousand meters altitude. "Bre'en. Give us another boost."

The Snowman opened his eyes, and looked dazedly out the hatch. For a moment Yoninne thought he was going to scream. Then he realized that their descent was relatively slow, and concentrated on the task Leg-Wot had set. Pulsing explosions of hypervelocity air sounded again above them. The chute pitched over to the west as the air rammed into it. Yoninne estimated that they were being dragged along at better than sixty meters per second—and as long as she kept the chute properly trimmed, much of that velocity was directed upward.

A minute passed and Leg-Wot motioned to the Snowman, who immediately stopped work. Relative quiet returned to the cabin. Four thousand meters, the altimeter said. *Not bad; even with all the ballast we're in good shape.* The dead oasis was lost in the morning glare. For the moment, all their problems lay within the skiff itself.

She trimmed the chute for maximum westward glide, and looked at the others. Bre'en was sunk down in his acceleration webbing, his eyes closed, apparently semiconscious. Crammed into the left side of the skiff, Pelio and Ajão looked uncomfortable but alert. As for Samadhom: the watchbear rested limply across her friends' laps, his massive head drooping over Pelio's knee. Every few seconds he swayed his head to the side, and a faint *meep* sounded from his hidden mouth. Poor fellow. If he had been human, she would have said he was sinking into delirium.

If Sam lost consciousness, then the tables would finally be turned—and Bre'en could kill them all. Then all the Snowman had to do was teleport the skiff back to the oasis, and he'd be home free. No, that wasn't quite right. They were several thousand meters up now—with all the potential energy that altitude gave them: unless Bre'en could find a rengable exchange mass, he would die of heatstroke teleporting down that far. But that was not an insuperable objection: if they were dead Bre'en could just wait until the parachute lowered the skiff to a safe altitude—and then "jump."

But did Bre'en know that? Did he really understand the chute's function? Perhaps she could convince him that without her cooperation, the skiff would fall like a rock. Her hand slid back to grasp the spill lanyard that hung close by the side of her webbing, hidden from Bre'en's view.

Seconds later, Bre'en groaned and sat a little straighter. Yoninne glanced quickly at the man, then pretended to concentrate on the trim stick in her left hand. "I want to show you something, Bre'en. You're not the only person needed to keep us in the air." She waited till she had his full attention, then released the stick from her left hand. At the same time, she surreptitiously yanked the spill lanyard with her right; in the olive dome above them, dozens of tiny vents slid open. The skiff's gentle descent became a swift free fall toward the desert below.

Pelio's eyes went wide. Bre'en gave a short barking yell, before trying madly to slow their fall. The Snowman teleported blast after blast at the chute, but it was close-reefed now and their fall continued. Yoninne waited, resisting the terrible urge to act, until the instant Bre'en seemed to realize that all his efforts were in vain. Then she made a great show of grabbing the stick, and pulling it quickly this way and that. Simultaneously, she reset the lanyard with her right hand, and prayed the chute would dereef.

It did, and their fall ended in a protracted *thunng* sound as

the shrouds stretched taut and the skiff resumed its eight-meter-per-second sink rate. Yoninne glanced at the skiff's simple instrument board. They had lost only two-hundred-meters' altitude; more surprising still, the whole game had lasted only seven seconds. She trimmed the chute back onto their original glide path, then fiddled impressively with the controls a few seconds more. Keeping her hand on the trim stick, she turned to Bre'en. "See what I mean?"

Thredegar Bre'en nodded dumbly. She noticed that Ajão's face was blank, an expression that Leg-Wot recognized as carefully concealed amusement.

They flew in silence for several minutes. Now the desert looked like tawny cement, littered with pebbles, splattered here and there with motor oil.

Gradually the land seemed to ripple. Long shadows stood the foothills up like great ridges. She leaned out past the hatch, into the wind: the mountains ahead rose a good thousand meters above them, the rounded summits speckled with trees, pepper on sand.

She had Bre'en give the craft another boost, and minutes later still another. Each time they drew swiftly closer to the mountains but each time they rose hundreds of meters. Yoninne swallowed again and again to ease the pressure in her ears.

They passed over the line of peaks, missing the nearest by less than five hundred meters. In the branches of the trees there, she saw tiny spots of color that must be flowers. But spectacular as it was, the land below them couldn't compare to what she saw over the mountains. The sea! A dark blue line along the western horizon. And the land between the mountains and the coast was green—not brown or ocher like the deserts behind them. The beautiful green band stretched as far to the north as she could see. So this was County Tsarang.

It was all downhill now; Bre'en had a much easier time of it. Yoninne estimated they could make it all the way to the coast if necessary. "Do you recognize any of this, Pelio?" she asked.

Pelio started to lean across Bre'en to look out the hatch. There were small observation windows slotted into the hull near him, but the open hatch provided a much better view. Samadhom shifted heavily across his lap and rolled limply against the wall. Pelio turned to cradle Sam's head in his arms. He looked back at Yoninne, and his voice quavered faintly. "Samadhom's still alive, I'm sure of it—"

But he's unconscious, thought Leg-Wot. Bre'en's attention flickered quickly from Yoninne to the watchbear and then back. *Thank God Bre'en thinks the skiff will fall without our help.*

Pelio reluctantly eased Sam onto the piled ballast, then returned to the hatch. He looked northward, then—gripping the edge of the hatch with both hands—leaned into the wind to look straight ahead. "We've done it, Ionina," he said softly. "The center of Tsarangalang city is just to the right of our path. It can't be more than a few miles away."

They grinned foolishly at each other for a moment. Then Pelio turned back to Samadhom.

Yoninne tipped the canopy slightly and the skiff angled off in the direction Pelio had indicated. They weren't more than two thousand meters up. The country below was wild by Homeworld standards, but Yoninne could see that it must be an Azhiri orchard. The greenery was speckled with red, and here and there she saw large stacks of the fruit waiting for transportation. An occasional building peeked through the foliage.

On the other side of the cabin, Pelio talked softly to Sam. Until the watchbear could be revived, the only thing that kept Bre'en from kenging them all was his fear of a crash. But that fear would diminish as the skiff sank nearer to earth.

Finally they were passing over the central districts of Tsarangalang: the buildings below were separated by scant hundreds of meters. Straight ahead lay the circular blue disk of the city's transit lake. That's where they'd have to touch down. With all the tons of ballast aboard, they were coming down so fast that Pelio and Ajão—unprotected by deceleration webbing—could get messed up if she landed on solid ground.

She arced wide around the lake trying to conserve every meter of altitude, trying to give Pelio and Samadhom more time. If necessary, she could force Bre'en to give the skiff still another boost. But what if Pelio couldn't bring Sam to? What if Sam were dying? She tried not to think about that possibility; they were so terribly close to success now.

Then a faint *meep* came from the furry hulk, and Pelio looked up triumphantly. Leg-Wot felt like howling with joy. She opened the spill flaps a trifle and the skiff sank toward the lake below at almost fourteen meters per second. She pushed the hatch all the way back and morning sunlight streamed over her shoulder into the cabin. The breeze whistling up around them brought the smells of green, growing things. *In just a few more seconds we'll be down there, safe.*

Four hundred meters up. Somehow a little sense crept through her euphoria. "Pelio," she said, "get between Samadhom and Bre'en, will you?" Before, threats had been sufficient to keep the Snowman in line; no doubt, Bre'en had been convinced of the hopelessness of the witlings' cause. But now that they were actually on the point of winning, he might try something desperate.

Pelio shifted Sam's weight onto Ajão, then turned to face Thredegar Bre'en. He steadied himself with one hand and held the machete in the other.

One hundred meters: Yoninne closed the spill flaps. She loosened her harness and leaned out the hatch, at the same time keeping her left hand on the trim stick. They were coming down near the edge of the lake—away from the piers—where she hoped the water was shallow; weighted down as it was, the skiff would float like a lead balloon.

Ashore, a crowd of locals stood gaping up at them; word travels fast in a society of teleports. If their wonder turned to fear they might shoot the skiff out of the sky.

The ground was so close now she could see single blades of grass growing between the stone blocks around the water's edge. She trimmed the chute across a microscopic updraft and estimated their sink rate at only six or seven meters per second. They'd strike the water more "gently" then a road boat coming out of a one-league jump.

Crump. The bolt of wind that slammed against the skiff was far too savage to be natural. Yoninne was pitched halfway out the hatch before the harness caught her. For an instant she thought some overanxious local had attacked them, but as she pulled herself back into the cabin, she saw that Pelio had fallen forward, that Bre'en had pinned his knife hand.

The Snowman kicked wildy at Sam and Ajão. Sam yelped twice and was silent. Bre'en hesitated just a second as he realized the animal was again impotent. Then he turned on Pelio.

"No!" screamed Yoninne as she lunged across the tiny space that separated them, her hands joined in a double fist. Bre'en twisted out of her way, and for what seemed an endless time his small eyes glared malevolently into hers.

Something exploded within her and she saw and felt and heard no more.

Nineteen

The Guildsman looked nothing like Thengets del Prou. Lan Mileru was a small man—even by Azhiri standards—and very old. The veins stood like a lace net across his round face, and his every motion was cautious, slow. Now he sat hunched over the map table, his rheumy eyes straining to follow the text of the letter before him.

From across the table, Pelio watched with a kind of desolate indifference. There hadn't been much life in the boy since Yoninne was—Ajão turned to look out the window, forceably supressing his line of thought.

Mileru's house was near the center of Tsarangalang. To the right Bjault could see the city's transit lake, and beyond it stood a room of the count's manse. There were only three or four other buildings in sight. Most were constructed of wood, the timbers worn and dry. Compared to the Summerkingdom, County Tsarang was arid and underpopulated. Only intense irrigation kept its orchards green. And apparently that irrigation system was one of the chief points of contention between the county and its Sandfolk neighbors.

Guildsman Mileru's veined and trembling hand slid Prou's letter back across the table to Ajão. "The letter is authentic, sir." He spoke with a thin, fragile voice. "Thengets del Prou's self-confident swagger is unmistakable. The boy is clever—and I don't mean simply Talented: I am inclined to believe what he says of you, fantastic though that be. And therefore, I must do the favor that he, and you, asked of me. When Count Dzeda is informed of the situation, I am sure that he will cooperate, too: the count is an honorable and imaginative man." *And a wild man, too*, thought Bjault. When they were pulled from the drowned skiff, it had been Count Dzeda who stood hip-deep in the water, shouting directions at his men. He acted more like a shop foreman than a nobleman—and his people didn't hesitate to talk back to him. Nevertheless, the rescue had been accomplished with dispatch.

"But," continued Lan Mileru, "is it really safe to take the injured woman? From what Thengets del Prou says, I do believe your people could pick her up later."

At this, Pelio gave Ajão a questioning look.

The Guildsman might have a point. *Yoninne*, thought Bjault, *will my scheme kill you? Or are you already dead?*

Just an hour earlier, they had left her in the count's manse, on the far side of the transit lake. There had been nothing they could do for the girl. She lay unmoving, her eyes closed, her breath barely detectable. The count's physician (perhaps "barber" or "faith healer" was a better title) had leaned over the space pilot to push back her eyelids.

"As you say, she is alive," the Azhiri doctor said. "But that is about all. Someone kenged her; it's a miracle she wasn't killed instantly. Perhaps she has some defenses against the Talent, even though you say she is a witling."

"No, it was Samadhom," Pelio said darkly, and reached under the couch to pet the animal's furry hulk. The prince-imperial had been kneeling beside Yoninne's body ever since she was brought in, but these were the first words he had added to the conversation.

Bjault looked down at the girl. Without her action there in the final seconds of the skiff's descent, Thredegar Bre'en could most likely have kenged them all—since the watchbear had been barely conscious after Bre'en kicked him in the face. But Yoninne had paid a high price in saving their lives: the tissues of her brain were torn and jumbled by Bre'en's tele-portive butchery. It was indeed a miracle, though perhaps an unhappy one, that her body continued to live.

Pelio broke the long silence that had followed his own re-mark. "Will . . . will she ever be herself again?" His tone was pleading.

"Your Highness, you know how rarely anyone is injured yet not killed by a keng attack. In fifteen years of Desertfolk raids, I've seen it happen only four times. In three of those cases the victim died within hours. In the fourth—well, the fourth fellow slowly wasted away, died without ever regain-ing his senses."

The physician had no theoretical expertise, but Ajão saw that he was right: either Yoninne's body would quickly die—like an engine without a governor—or else it would continue to function till it starved to death. If the first, then the jump to Draere's island could do her no harm. And if the second, then she had everything to gain by going. Most likely, Draere had left a first-aid cache at the telemetry station; that was the usual procedure at stations that might be revisited in the future. There would be drugs there, perhaps even intravenous feeding equipment. He could keep Yoninne's body alive till rescue came, till competent medics had a chance to resurrect her mind.

The thought brought him back to the present, and Lan Mileru's questioning gaze. "She'll make the jump along with Prince Pelio and myself."

They were interrupted by the sounds of splashing water. Two men wearing kilts of county blue climbed from the room's transit pool. "Gentlemen," the taller of the two announced, "the Count of —"

Before he reached the word "Tsarang," Dzeru Dzeda bounced out of the water.

"Hello, Lan," the count said, and waved dismissal at the servants. Dzeda was a tall Azhiri, his skin almost as dark a gray as Thengets del Prou's. Bjault guessed the fellow had more than a few ancestors in common with the Desertfolk that were his land's traditional enemies. The nobleman had been quite a surprise. County Tsarang was a backwater of the Summerkingdom, and Ajão had expected its ruler to be either haughtily officious, like the prefect of Bodgaru, or else cautious and mousy, like the consul at Grechper. But Dzeda was neither. Apparently his position here did not amount to exile from the court of Summer: his family had been running this part of the world long before the Summerkingdom extended its influence here.

The count walked across the room to greet Pelio and Bjault with a certain courteous flippancy. "I would have been here with you, but I was called to the East Line. Do you know, I think the Snowking has half his army sitting in transit lakes out there? I've never seen the like of it; I'll bet they even have their Desertfolk friends scared. The Snowmen accuse you and the kenged girl of trying to assassinate King Tru'ud, and they demand we give you up. I offered to return Bre'en instead, but that just seemed to make them angrier. They're blockading the Island Road until we give in to them."

"If they make open war on you," said Lan Mileru, "you'll have the Guild on your side." There was steel in his quavering voice. "The last group that fought the Guild no longer exists."

"I know," said Dzeda. "And that's what I told their envoys. They must be terribly desperate." He turned to eye Ajão speculatively. "And I think I know why. It's not simply that old Tru'ud got his kilt mussed. . . .

"That was a remarkable device you flew here this morning, Adgao. From what we've been able to get out of Bre'en, I see that it's a trick we can duplicate. Just think: with such fliers, pilgrims need never again risk boating across even the shortest stretch of open sea. And soldiers can penetrate enemy territory without ever setting foot on it. What other secrets do you and the girl have, Adgao? I do believe the Snowmen think you could make them stronger than the Guild itself." He cocked his head to one side. "Could you really?"

Ajão ignored the tiny cramp that was gnawing at his middle. "Not by ourselves," he said. "But perhaps, if my people and yours were to meet, they could teach each other a thing or two."

"Hmm." Dzeda plunked himself down on the upholstered bench that ran around the map table. "I suppose you've told Lan of your adventures," he said to Pelio, "and this suicidal plan you have for renging across the ocean."

The elderly Guildsman smiled. "More than that, dear My Lord. I intend to cooperate with them."

"What!"

"That's right," Mileru said. On the map between them he pointed at Draere's island, three-quarters of the way around the equator from County Tsarang. "At their convenience, I will teleport them here."

"Why, blood and bile, Lan. You're as crazy as they are! That's more than one hundred and twenty-five leagues. A four-league jump is enough to shatter the hull of the toughest road boat. We can't even reng message balls more than twenty leagues without risking their contents." He all but bounced off the bench in his agitation.

Lan Mileru seemed to be enjoying the other's consternation. "Nevertheless, Dzeru, I have been convinced they should be allowed to try." He held out Prou's letter.

But Dzeda waved it aside. "If you three are so eager to smear yourselves across that speck of mud out in the ocean," he said to Ajão, "why did you bother coming to County Tsarang? Why not have some Guildsman reng you there direct from the Summerpalace? The palace is closer to the island than Tsarang. And there are places in the Snowkingdom that are still closer: I'll bet if you made the jump from Ga'arvi, you'd crash into your destination 'gently' enough to leave recognizable corpses."

Ajão smiled at the other's sarcasm. "There is a reason for coming to your county, My Lord. If we make the jump from here, we will be thrown upward from the ground at our destination." The problem was not especially difficult to visualize. Imagine the planet spinning on its axis, a vast, spherical merry-go-round in space. The Summerpalace was just ninety degrees east of Draere's island; if they jumped from the palace they'd be smashed into the ground when they emerged at the telemetry station. Ga'arvi was a better prospect (except that it was a Snowfolk town). Renging to the telemetry station from there would be like hopping from the center of a merry-go-round straight out to the edge: they would arrive moving due west—at nearly the speed of sound. Yoninne had dismissed Ga'arvi with the comment, "Who wants to make a belly landing at mach one?"

But as you followed the continent from Ga'arvi to the isthmus of Tsarang, the situation improved. If they jumped to Draere's island from Tsarangalang, they would arrive moving better than a kilometer per second—but that velocity would be directed upward at almost 23 degrees. The only better jumping-off point in either hemisphere was the east coast of the isthmus, but that was under Desertfolk control, and besides, there was no Guildsman there.

"I realize," Bjault continued, "that our boat might still crash into something—a steep hillside or cliff face, for instance—but this is about the best we can do, given the arrangement of Giri's continents."

Dzeda shook his head despairingly. "No. You'll die in any case. Don't you realize that when air moves fast enough, it might as well be solid rock? I've seen men and war boats struck by air renged from sixty leagues: the men spattered, and the boats were turned to kindling. Your boat may be strong, but nothing can resist forces like that."

Ajão started to disagree, but the count raised his hand. "Let me finish. I know Shozheru has put you under what amounts to a suspended death sentence. Either you go through with this plan or he executes the three of you. But you're in County Tsarang now. We were an independent state long before there even was a Summerkingdom. Back at the palace they may call me count and vassal—but out here that's not quite the way things are: I am willing to grant you a secret asylum, to report to the Summerkingdom that you went through with your plan. Frankly, I think this is what your father was aiming at when he agreed to this scheme, Pelio. His advisers may be cold men, but he is not.

"How about it? Will you stay?"

Ajão was silent. For Yoninne and himself there was no choice. Unless they could get to the telemetry station and call in a rescue ship from Novamerika, they would die—and soon. Already he was beginning to feel the same pain and weakness he had on the trip to Grechper.

Pelio *did* have a choice. Dzeru Dzeda's offer finally took him off the deadly hook that Ajão and Prou and Yoninne had forced him onto. Perhaps their machinations wouldn't ruin the boy's life, after all.

But the young prince looked from Bjault to Dzeda, and then slowly shook his head. "I want to be with . . . I mean, I want to go with Adgao and Ionina."

The count saw the refusal in Ajão's face, too. He pursed his lips, and for a moment seemed lost in minute inspection of the floor between his feet. There was a wan smile on his face as he looked back at Ajão. "Well, I tried, good witling. You may never know how scared I am: scared of what might happen if you fall into unfriendly hands; scared of what your people may do to us if you bring them back here. My race has always depended on its natural Talent—while yours apparently has none: you've had to substitute ingenuity and invention for Talent. Somehow, I suspect that's taken your people much, much further than mine have come."

Something turned to ice in Bjault's spine: this petty nobleman could destroy their last hope for rescue if he chose.

But Dzeda bounced to his feet, and some of his cheerful nature returned. "But at the same time, I'm overburdened with soft-heartedness. And curiosity. If your insane scheme works, the future could be an interesting place, indeed.

"Give them whatever they need, Lan," he said over his shoulder, as he walked to the transit pool. "I'll be out on the East Line the next few hours, keeping watch on our unfriendly neighbors."

———

Through the wide windows of the count's manse, Ajão could see bands of orange and green the setting sun had spread above the ocean to the west, while the mountains in the east were barely darker than the sky there. The warm bluish twilight that filled the gardens about the manse was infinitely cheerful compared to the stark light and dark they had traveled through at the poles.

Bjault shook his head, trying to concentrate on the fiberene chute that was spread around him. The temptation to quit, to get some sleep, was overpowering. But he knew that part of his fatigue was not natural. Every time he smiled into a mirror he saw the line of blue along his gums. The pain in his gut was getting steadily worse, much as it had on the trip to Grechper. Only this time he might not recover from the attack. If they didn't make the jump soon, there was a good chance he would be too sick to guide the skiff to a landing once they reached Draere's island.

Dzeda's men had moved the skiff into the manse's meeting hall. It sat on the marble floor, and all around it lay the parachute's olive fabric. Across the room, Pelio and the others worked to remove every fleck of dirt from the slick material.

But folding the parachute was something which only he, Ajão Bjault, could do. The packing pattern was intricate, and each of the canopy's movable flaps had to be specially accounted for; a single mistake could be fatal. As the minutes passed, the ache in his tired arms became a pulsing fire. Soon he needed Pelio's help to compact the mass he had folded.

Early in the afternoon, Ajão had briefly considered a plan that didn't require the chute to be repacked: if they could get a Tsarangi volunteer, perhaps they could *fly* the skiff across the ocean, the same way Bre'en had flown them over the mountains. But Draere's island was nearly twenty thousand kilometers away, and Lan Mileru pointed out that even a two- or three-man *team* of teleports couldn't keep the skiff airborne for the hundreds of hours it would take to fly that distance.

So they must stick to the original scheme: Lan would teleport them across the ocean in a single jump; they'd slam up into the air over Draere's island at better than a kilometer per second, fast enough to rip even a fiberene chute to shreds. Only when their speed fell well below mach one could they pop the chute and sink "gently" to a landing.

Suddenly Bjault stopped work, stared blankly at the pile before him. His mind had wandered; what was next? Back in the Summerpalace, he made Yoninne show him every step of the folding process. She had considered the demand a waste of time, but now the memory of what he had seen there was all he had to guide him.

Yoninne, girl, what I wouldn't give to have you here swearing at me. Only now did he realize what an effective team they had made. Again and again he'd come up with a good idea, and Yoninne would somehow put together all the details to make it work.

The last colors of sunset had faded when Pelio and Dzeda's men squeezed the chute into its retaining straps. The fabric no longer looked fragile and gauzy. Ajão's careful work had transformed it into a thick, dark slab that massed nearly as much as an equivalent volume of rock.

While Ajão and Lan watched, the younger men lifted the pack and set it in the rectangular slot at the top of the skiff. Then Bjault closed the cowling over the chute and crawled through the passenger hatch into the vehicle. He moved slowly now, his body bent. The pain in his middle made it all but impossible to think. For a moment he lay quivering in the darkness—then Pelio called to him, and someone held a torch in front of the hatchway. Ajão gagged on the oily smoke, and forced himself upright. "I'm all right," he said to the men outside. Back to work: he connected the chute release, then briefly checked the cords holding the lead ballast in place. *Finished*. He crawled out of the skiff, and stood swaying on the marble floor. "Lan, we're ready. You can jump us in four hours." That would be the middle of the night here—but morning at Draere's island.

Even by the flickering torchlight, Ajão could see real concern on the old Guildsman's face. "Perhaps you should wait. Just a day or two."

"No!" Ajão opened his mouth, tried to put his reasons into words, but all he knew was the pain in his middle. The floor swung up toward his face, and everything turned black. He didn't feel Pelio's arms break his fall.

As it happened, Bjault's wishes prevailed, even though he was not awake to argue for them: the Snowmen attacked shortly after midnight.

Twenty

Ajão struggled to wakefulness, trying ineffectually to shake off the hands on his shoulders. From all around him came the crash of thunder—and something that sounded terribly like small-arms fire. He forced his eyes open and looked blearily at the shadowed face above him.

The count's voice was barely intelligible over the noise outside: "Blood and bile, good witling, I was beginning to think nothing would stir you—Lan, he's awake—" He shouted the words over his shoulder, then turned back to the Novamerikan. "We've got to get out of here, and fast. Can you walk?"

Bjault came cautiously to his feet, but felt little of the earlier pain. Only now did he see the extent of the disaster that was falling about them. Across the room, Pelio and Mileru were helping county troops slip Yoninne onto a stretcher. Less than three meters from her feet, the thick wood wall lay in shattered ruin. From the moonlit landscape beyond, the sounds of destruction continued. "What's happening?" he shouted to Dzeda, but a thunderclap blotted out his words. He let the count push him into the room's transit pool, along with the other witlings and Samadhom.

A second later they emerged in the meeting hall of the county manse. This was several kilometers from the bedrooms, and the sounds of combat were muted here. A moon shone through the room's crystal windows; the soldiers standing around the water looked pale and worried. Ajão repeated his question, and this time Dzeda replied, "—tried to surprise us. There are a few Sandfolk who have made the pilgrimage to the Tsarangalang transit lake. They are being used to reng the Snowman army into the city. I'll bet Tru'ud thought if he hit us hard enough he could capture or kill you two before we could react—and he was almost right."

A nearby soldier interrupted. "The messengers say they've got roadblocks on nearly every lake within three leagues, M'Lord."

Dzeda frowned, and said to Lan Mileru, "What do you seng?"

"I think he's right, Dzeru. The lakes are quite turbulent."

"Very well. We'll pull back. If the Snowfolk keep this up, I'll be asking for Guild assistance."

"You'll have it," Lan replied.

The count gave instructions to a squad of messengers, then turned to Ajão and Pelio. "By the monsters in the sea, Tru'ud is risking everything to get his hands on you. And as long as you're in the county he stands a fair chance of succeeding. Adgao . . . are you up to going through with your plan right now?"

Bjault looked down at Yoninne's still form on the litter. Pelio said, "She's no worse than before, Adgao." Outside, the crack and rip of war sounded louder. He looked at the count and nodded. The pain in his gut had diminished—though not as completely as at Grechper. This was the best chance they would ever have.

"Good. Lan?"

"I'm ready, Dzeru." They walked across the hall to the ablation skiff. The Guildsman had the soldiers turn the skiff to the compromise attitude he and Ajão had decided on: something Mileru could manage, that would leave the skiff's center of mass roughly in line with their direction of flight when they emerged at Draere's island; otherwise, the hypersonic entry would put them in a spin that would rip the interior ballast from its moorings and splatter them to pulp. But the skiff was so small and dense that the troopers had a hard time getting leverage on it. And the further it was tipped to the side, the more dangerous its tendency to roll.

They had finally wedged the skiff in place, when a ripping stutter of explosions—like automatic gunfire—traced across the meeting hall's upper windows. Around them, the troopers dropped to the floor. Dzeda shouted into his ear, "Get down! They're renging rocks."

They fell to their bellies and crawled around to the west side of the skiff. "One nice thing about living at the equator," the count continued, "is that renged projectiles must always come out of the east."

In the moonlit night they heard screams mixed with the staccato impacts. A soldier crawled swiftly across the floor to them. "Dzeda! Snowfolk squads are moving in our direction from the lake."

Crump. An immense crash sounded from down the hillside.

"I doubt they know where the witlings are," said Mileru, "but if their reconnaissance squads get this far—"

"—They'll reng in whole companies, and we'll be overrun," Dzeda finished. "But see here, Lan, I've ordered the area around the lake evacuated. I want Guild assistance to wipe out the forces there. That will give us time to finish what we have to do here."

The frail, aged Guildsman was silent for a long moment, then spoke agreement—to what, Ajão didn't discover till a couple of seconds later:

Pearly light shone through the west windows, silhouetting the ridge line that separated them from the main transit lake. The hall was briefly lit as bright as day, and the moon seemed insignificantly pale. As the light began to fade toward crimson, the ground beneath them jolted and danced; the skiff rocked gently where it sat, but the calks held. Lan said, "A rock from the outer moon, perhaps one hundred tons in weight . . . I renged it down to the transit lake." Ajão looked at the Guildsman, but saw no sign of triumph in his old face.

Then the shock wave—refracted and attenuated by its passage over the ridge line—slammed against the meeting hall. The west wall bulged inward like some arthritic curtain, then crashed across the marble floor. The timbers above them first lifted, then settled lopsidedly.

Bjault watched, his jaw sagging: one hundred tons, the Guildsman said. One hundred tons, renged down through 200,000 kilometers. The potential energy released would be on the order of a small fission bomb. And the palsied Guildsman could bring such destruction to any point in the world. Tru'ud must be desperate indeed to risk such retaliation.

Dzeda was already on his feet. "Hurry. Lan's wiped out the force at the lake, but there are still enemy scouts in our area, and if there's any water left in the lake—"

"There isn't," Lan said sadly, almost to himself.

"—They might try to reestablish a roadhead."

In the ringing silence, Ajão and Pelio opened the skiff's hatch and helped fit Yoninne into her acceleration webbing. It was strange to see her face so peaceful and composed, while Armageddon itself played around them. Beyond the ruined wall, dust rose shimmering into the moonlight, softening the outlines of the wrecked buildings down the hillside. The scene might have been out of the Last Interregnal War on Homeworld, the aftermath of an aerial bombing. Yet there was no sign of smoke or fire. Except for Lan's weapon, all the destruction had been done by wind and cold stone.

Bjault climbed aboard the skiff, and settled into his harness. Pain was beginning to pulse through his middle again—this latest recovery had been the briefest yet. He looked back through the hatchway to see Pelio turn aside from Dzeda and Lan.

"Here, Samadhom," the boy said. The watchbear crawled awkwardly across the debris-strewn floor to his master. Pelio knelt and held the animal's large head in his arms. "Goodby, Samadhom," he said softly, voice quavering.

The watchbear could not come with them on this trip. The skiff's acceleration webbing could protect two—at most three—passengers. That hadn't mattered much during their relatively gentle flight with Bre'en over the mountains, but when the witlings slammed into the air at Draere's island, the initial deceleration would amount to more than twenty gravities. Dzeda was right in a way: when you strike air at hypersonic speeds, it *is* something like a stone wall. Sam would die if they took him along.

But Sam understood none of this; as Pelio climbed into the skiff, the creature bumbled frantically after. Dzeda caught him by the shoulders and pulled him back; Sam's *meeping* was weak but desperate. Pelio leaned out of the skiff and said, "Please, good Dzeru, will you care well for him?"

For once the count's face was absolutely serious. "I will." He looked back into the cabin at Bjault and added significantly, "I will keep him in good health . . . in expectation that you will return."

Dzeda stepped back from the hatchway, and Bjault conferred one last time with Lan Mileru. Then the hatch was shut, secured—and they were alone. Through the window slits, Ajão watched the others depart; no one wanted to be anywhere near when the skiff jumped. As Bjault and the Guildsman had planned it, the skiff would emerge about a hundred meters above the ground near Draere's station, which itself was three hundred meters above sea level; conservation of energy was not violated, however, since Tsarangalang stood at least four hundred meters above sea level. But the air they displaced over Draere's island would be renged back here—to emerge moving at better than a kilometer per second. Woe betide anyone standing in the way.

The silence stretched on. Ajão had hoped that there would be no time in these last seconds for thought, for fear. As long as this moment had been days away, he could regard the plan as a simple problem in aerodynamics—one that math and common sense could solve. But now he was staking their lives on that solution, and the risks that he and Yoninne had glossed over could not be ignored: they might as well be sailing the ocean in a leaky rubber raft, or falling over a cataract in a wooden barrel. The skiff had been designed to fly at speeds far greater than a thousand meters per second—but only above the stratosphere, through air ten thousand times thinner than at sea level. Even with all the ballast they were carrying, the dense lower atmosphere would generate twenty gravities of drag. Could the hull and the ballast restraints take that? After all, the skiff was primarily intended to sustain thermal stress—not high-gee loadings.

Ping. Pingping. The skiff jiggled slightly against its calking blocks. Ajão looked across the dark cabin at Pelio. "Someone's renging stones again," the boy said. A muffled explosion sounded from overhead and the ruined ceiling sagged even lower toward the skiff. Through the narrow windows he saw soldiers moving in the moonlight, soldiers who wore heavy leggings instead of Summer kilts.

Lan, reng us out of here! prayed Bjault.

And the prayer was answered: one instant Ajão hung loosely from his harness, and the next—the next, he was squashed back in the webbing, and the skin on his face and arms tried to slide from his bones. In one crushing blow, the air was forced from his lungs and no more would enter. The wavering haze of blackout closed in upon his mind. . . .

. . . But not before he saw, through the window slits, a sunlit morning horizon falling away above them.

Twenty-one

As soon as the Council meeting ended, Bjault returned to the hospital.

Hospital Main was typical colonial architecture: a one-story building molded from fused alumina, with every door and every window manual. It was both practical and unlovely. But the Novamerikans had put their medical center on Oceanside Grade, overlooking the pyramidal palms and pink beaches that edged the polar sea. And of all the buildings in the new colony, the hospital was the only one with landscaped grounds. As Ajão walked across the deeply sodden lawn, the smells of flowers and grass mixed with those of the alien ocean. It was evening. The sun skidded along the horizon in a kind of extended sunset, its light turning the breaking waves to gold and translucent green. Here at the Novamerikan South Pole it would be evening—or something like evening—for another forty days. Then the sun would set and the winter storms begin. They weren't as bad as the summer's, when the sea came close to boiling, but they were bad enough; without special protection this lawn might drown in the rains.

He stepped off the grass and onto the ruby-tiled walk that led indoors. Bjault had spent the last thirty days in this building. For most of that time he was unconscious, his body's blood replaced by a synthetic hydrocarbon that provided just enough oxygen to keep him alive while it slowly leached the metallic poisons from his tissues. The doctors told him that when the rescue ferry landed at Draere's island, he was already deep in a necrotic coma. The last thing Ajão remembered was sitting in the transmission shack at the telemetry station, talking half-deliriously into a jury-rigged mike—and receiving no answer. Survival had been a close thing indeed.

But the rescue had meant more than individual survival. He could see that in the faces of the medical technicians who greeted him along the hallway. They had watched the Council meeting on the two-way; they realized that these last few days would change the course of man's history through all space.

Bjault stopped at the door marked "10" and knocked softly. A moment passed, and Pelio-nge-Shozheru, the first Azhiri ever to leave his native planet, opened the door. The boy smiled shyly. "Hello, Ajão," he said in Homespeech, even doing a creditable job with the word "Ajão." Then he reverted to his own language. "I was hoping you would have time to visit us."

Bjault stepped inside and looked across the room. And his spirits sank for a moment into his boots. Yoninne Leg-Wot lay asleep, the crisp blue hospital sheets drawn carefully up to her throat. An IV bulb hung at the head of the bed, though Ajão had heard that she was physically capable of taking solid foods.

They sat down on the bed. Ajão didn't know quite what to say. Somehow, it hurt to look at the girl's peaceful face. He turned to the former prince. "Are they treating you well?"

Pelio nodded. "Your folk are kind, though very inquisitive. *My* Talent is scarcely measurable: you should see all the tests Thengets del Prou is going through." Again that shy smile. "On the other hand, I'm learning from them, too. And they're going to bring Samadhom back on the next trip to Giri; they're almost as eager to see him as I."

He rested his hand on the bandages that swathed Leg-Wot's head. "Best of all, Ionina is improving steadily. She wakes several times a day, and she recognizes me—I even think she understands what I say. Your doctors are really very good."

Ajão grunted noncommittally. *Yoninne*, he thought, looking at her still form on the bed, *if only you could know how very much your sacrifice will mean eventually*. He himself hadn't known for sure, till three days before, when he had heard Egr Gaun raging at the med tech just outside his hospital room.

"God damn it, woman," the science adviser's voice had carried clearly through the supposedly soundproofed wall. "I'm going to talk to him; I know he's awake and alert. NOW LET ME BY!" The door crashed open and Gaun stalked across the room to Bjault's bed. "How are you, Aj, old man?" he said, then turned to glare back through the doorway. The tech quietly shut the door, and the two men were alone. Gaun muttered something about "obstreperous red tape" and grinned conspiratorially at the archaeologist. As usual, the man's behavior left Bjault in a faint daze. Gaun was a competent mathematician, and he understood the mechanics of administration, but most often he relied on sheer bluster to get his way. He was just the man Ajão had been hoping to see.

"Now that you're awake, I thought you'd want to know what we've been doing with your discoveries."

Bjault nodded eagerly.

"That was quite a story you beamed us from Draere's station. Part of the Council thought you were simply delirious, but the rest voted to go through with the contact scheme you proposed: Ferry 03 picked up this Thengets del Prou shortly after we had you safely in orbit aboard the 02.

"Since we got back, we've put Prou through every test the labs can handle. We still haven't the foggiest idea how the fellow does it, but we do know that his trick conserves all the usual quantities—excepting angular momentum."

Ajão shrugged. He would have been astounded if *both* angular and linear momentum were conserved during teleportation.

Gaun continued slyly, "There is, however, one other bit of conventional wisdom that our Azhiri friends have bent badly out of shape. When the lab people were done with Prou here on the ground, we took him into space on the 03; turns out he can teleport the ferry up to 400,000 kilometers in a single jump. . . . But just guess how long it takes him to do that."

Ajão silently damned the man for keeping him in suspense. "How long?"

"To the clocks aboard the 03, no time at all; to the clocks here on the ground, about 1.2 milliseconds." The science adviser settled back to enjoy the expression on Bjault's face. He was not disappointed. "That's more than a thousand times the speed of light," Ajão said softly. Ever since he and Yoninne had learned of the Azhiri Talent, this had been the fantastic, incredible hope at the back of his mind. But still: "What about causality? With faster-than-light travel, you can create situations where—"

"—Where an effect precedes its own cause?" Gaun finished the sentence for him. "Right. That's always been the basic reason why people have accepted the light barrier. But now that we have a demonstrable ftl drive—namely Thengets del Prou—we're forced to come up with some explanation, be it ever so unaesthetic. For example, suppose teleportation is instantaneous—in some particular frame of reference, independent of the teleport's motion. Then effect could be made to precede cause, but only where the interval separating cause from effect is spacelike. See—no paradoxes."

"You're conjecturing some kind of 'super-luminiferous ether'?"

Gaun nodded. "Kinda sticks in your craw, don't it?"

Not really. Bjault had spent much of his life digging physics out of libraries buried in the ruins of ancient cities; that's why they called him an archaeologist. Yet he always dreamed of finding something that was totally new to man's experience. "You may be right, Egr. We should ask Prou to jump test probes in different directions. If there's an 'ether drift,' that—"

Gaun waved his hand airily. "Sure, Aj, we're doing all that. But look: what we really want is to duplicate and improve upon the Azhiri trick, to build ships that can travel between the stars in days instead of decades. We've gotta find out what goes on inside Prou's head when he teleports, and to do that we need a lot more equipment than some clocks and a planetary ferry. We need biophysics labs, and a few thousand topnotch specialists—things we don't have on Novamerika.

"I want to break the ramscoop out of mothballs, and fly

an Azhiri volunteer back to Homeworld, where such facilities *do* exist."

Gaun seemed almost intimidated by his own suggestion. It wasn't that they couldn't find an Azhiri willing to spend years in cold-sleep on a trip between the stars: Prou, at least, was so basically Faustian that he'd be eager to go. But the million-ton starship that had brought the colonists from Homeworld was partially dismantled now, much of its equipment built into Novamerikan ground installations. It would take a major effort to refit the ship, and the colony would be weakened as a result. Ajão said as much to Gaun.

"I know, and that's the real reason why I've come to you," admitted the science adviser. "The Council isn't going to like my idea one bit, and if I try to ram it down their throats like I have some things in the past, they're gonna like it even less. But you they respect, even admire. You're so damn diffident— and so damn right most of the time—that if you told the Council to go to blazes, they'd probably ask you the way.

"I want you to present my case to the Council. Tell them how much the colony will eventually gain again from this sacrifice. Sure, we'll be set back a couple decades—even if we refit the starship for a minimum payload—but when the first ftl ship arrives from Homeworld, we'll make it all back, and more. Will you tell them, Aj?"

Bjault had agreed, and when the time came, he spoke before the Council, which put the matter to a general referendum over the two-way. The vote had not been close: in less than a year's time, Thengets del Prou, Ajão Bjault, and a dozen others would begin the forty-year voyage to Homeworld.

. . . But Yoninne Leg-Wot would remain here, perhaps forever unaware of what she had made possible. The thought brought him back to the present, to the hospital room, to Pelio and Yoninne. He suddenly saw that the girl's eyes were open, and had been for several seconds. There was self-awareness in those eyes, but none of the fire and determination he had known.

"Hello," the girl said. "My name is Ionina. Who are you?" Her voice was calm, peaceful. But she spoke in the language of the Summerkingdom, and pronounced her own name the queer, unpalatalized way Pelio did.

Bjault replied, but Yoninne said nothing more; though her eyes remained open, she seemed to lose interest in her surroundings. Pelio looked up from the girl, his face alight. "Did you hear her, Ajão! The doctors were right. She will recover!"

He tried to respond to the boy's enthusiasm, but failed. When Bjault first regained consciousness, he had asked about Yoninne. "She'll definitely improve," the medic had said. "I don't see any reason why she won't eventually be able to take care of herself, talk, even write. But most of her memory has been wiped away, and it's possible that she will never again be able to reason at the highest levels of abstraction."

So. Their adventure on Giri had given him the stars—and taken from her the essence of her individuality. Somehow, it hurt to think of both at the same time. . . .

———

She was glad when the stranger left. She vaguely realized that he belonged somewhere in the vanished past, with all the memories, skills, and experience that had made her a different person. But that other she had suffered much, and had never really enjoyed herself. Now there was another chance.

She looked up at Pelio's gray-green face, and took his thick hand in hers. She had lost much that was of value, but she was no fool. She knew a happy ending when she found one.

About the Author

Vernor Vinge is a four-time Hugo Award winner (for the novels *A Deepness in the Sky* and *A Fire Upon the Deep* and the novellas "Fast Times at Fairmont High" and "The Cookie Monster") and a four-time Nebula Award finalist. He has been featured in such diverse venues as *Rolling Stone, Wired, The New York Times, Esquire,* and NPR's "Fresh Air." His most recent novel is *Rainbows End*.

Highly regarded by scientists, journalists, business leaders—as well as readers—for his concept of the technological singularity, Vinge has spoken all over the world on scientific subjects. For many years a mathematician and computer science professor at San Diego State University, he's now a full-time author. He lives in San Diego, California.